TEMPTATION
SHIFTERS FOREVER WORLDS

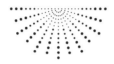

ELLE THORNE

Thank you for reading!

*To receive exclusive updates from Elle Thorne and to be the
first to get your hands on the next release,
please sign up for her newsletter.
Put this in your browser:
http://www.ellethorne.com/contact*

Copyright © 2016 by Elle Thorne

All rights reserved.

No part of this book may be reproduced in any form or by any electronic or mechanical means, including information storage and retrieval systems, without written permission from the author, except for the use of brief quotations in a book review.

TEMPTATION

Joe's got a problem. There's a curvy bear shifter trespassing in Bear Canyon Valley. And he's been charged with taking care of the matter.

Looks like he's got two problems, because he didn't count on wanting her.

She's a curvy bear shifter that wants to be left alone. Tell that to Joe.

Visit www.ElleThorne.com to sign up for Elle's newsletter!

ELLE THORNE

CHAPTER ONE

Joe knew shifters. He knew their ways. He'd been around shifters all his life. He trusted shifters and they trusted him back. His best friend Grant was a shifter. Joe's grandfather's best friend was Grant's grandfather, also a bear shifter. Joe wasn't a shifter, but he felt like his family was, especially here in Bear Canyon Valley, where the shifters were a tight bunch.

Nothing about shifters surprised Joe much. He'd not seen many female shifters. Most of them were male, at least the ones that Joe knew.

As much as Joe trusted shifters, one thing he didn't yield to was temptation. The temptation to be mated to a shifter. He kept his distance emotionally when it came to shifter females. They loved hard. Passionately. That kind of emotion made Joe nervous.

Joseph Dark—originally, Joseph Dark Eagle Rises

After Winter Storm—who now went by Joe Dark, held his breath, fighting to keep his pulse under control. He kept the fragrant, familiar air he'd sucked in locked tight in his lungs. He knew the air and the terrain here as well as he knew every scar and every broken bone on his body.

A tiny rivulet of sweat made its way down his back, creeping toward the waistband on the jeans he filled out, front and back. He itched to scratch the tickling trickle.

He'd used hunter's block today. He'd never used it when he was looking for her before. He hadn't wanted to deceive her, but now that he'd been assigned by the clan to the task of reconnoitering and discovering more about her, he felt a bit of stealth would serve the cause better. The Bear Canyon Valley clan wanted to be sure she wasn't a threat.

She.

The female bear shifter.

Joe had agreed to look into the female bear shifter who roamed Bear Canyon Valley because he'd brought her food a couple of times. He knew she'd scented him, but as long as he kept his distance, she'd never given more than a snort to acknowledge his presence.

The female had a shifter cub with her. If she'd thought he was a threat, he was certain he wouldn't be alive anymore. Female bears were extremely protective.

Today, his visit to the forest she frequented was different. Now he had a different purpose.

Joe hadn't been completely honest with the clan when they'd brought her up to him. He'd hinted that he knew of her existence in a cursory way. This wasn't exactly true. Joe didn't regret his deception, because he knew the moment he yielded the truth he'd be subjected to an assortment of questions and then ribbing about her.

He sat in the tree, as high up as he could get, and watched the forest floor below. He'd brought her food, as he'd done a couple of times before.

Food for her and the cub. The little tyke would scramble out of the cover of the trees and head for the decadent aroma the food put out. Usually Joe would bring pot roast or ham, or even a turkey.

The female would eat whatever was left over after she let the little one indulge.

But she never shifted. Joe had no idea what she looked like as a human. Why didn't she shift? Shifters—at least the ones Joe knew—preferred to be in their human form. Why didn't she?

He heard a tiny crunching sound. The food he'd placed at the base of a tree three yards away from the one that he was in had to be hard to resist when you were a hungry baby bear. Not that the woods weren't full of food, but shifters typically gravitated toward human food.

Sure enough, a dark brown figure scampered out

from between a couple of trees to the west. The little one snorted its delight, growling and snarling gleefully.

A louder, more ferocious growl joined his. There she was. She was magnificent. Queenly, with a presence that commanded respect and even fear, for some. She followed the cub, her dark eyes alert, her head tilted, always on her guard. Joe knew mama bears. He knew shifter mamas too. It seemed excessive, as if she was on the lookout for something specific.

Was it him? Was she worried about him? How could she be? He'd only known about her a couple of weeks now. She followed the little one until she reached the tree Joe was in.

She stopped suddenly, watching the cub eat, but her head was cocked to the side. Listening. Listening to what?

The bear cub ravaged the ham Joe had brought, tearing into it, shredding it with his claws, swallowing chunks. Joe fought the smile that threatened to make an appearance. He needed to maintain control over his emotions so that she couldn't notice the change with her bear senses and pick up his pulse.

He breathed a shallow breath of relief and looked back at her.

Shit.

Busted.

She was staring at him, her bear head raised, her

eyes focused on him directly. He had no doubt he was the cause of the intensity in her gaze.

Oh, hell, here goes nothing.

"Well, if you know I'm here, you may as well talk to me," Joe told her. "And you can clearly see I'm not armed." He tried to convince her he wasn't a threat.

The cub paused, looked at its mother, then at Joe, and went back to its meal.

Joe heard a low, rumbling sound that came from deep within her chest.

"No. No growling. No bear talk. I know damned well what you are. I mean talk to me like a human."

She scratched at the ground with her large, sharp claws.

"What if I promise not to come down?"

A creaking and a light crunching sound, and a moment later he saw the woman in her emerging and her bear receding.

CHAPTER TWO

Oh, damn. She had no clothing. But when Grant shifted and was fully dressed. Joe fought with confusion and something else...

That something else, he realized immediately, was the temptation to look at her. He couldn't conquer it. Joe feasted his eyes on the woman in front of him.

She stood proudly, her hands on her hips, her chest thrust forward, her jaw set with a determination Joe hadn't seen in many people.

She was magnificent. A warrior. A woman. A shifter. A bear. Completely naked and glorious in her woman form.

Her skin was a light mocha color, and she had curves on top of curves. Her hips were full, and her thighs blossomed out from the full hips. They were luscious. Her hips narrowed to her waist, then flared out again, revealing full breasts, dark nipples erect.

Joe's anatomy responded in exactly the way he wished it wouldn't. Nature's telltale way of exhibiting his arousal. He grew hard in his pants, and his pulse raced, the blood traveling through his veins felt like it was being propelled by jet fuel. He swallowed hard, and wanted to avert his eyes but couldn't.

Her own dark brown gaze pierced him, showing no shame and no shyness. She wasn't aroused; she wasn't anything but this amazing, proud creature completely comfortable in her skin and at ease with the knowledge she could and would do whatever she needed to defend herself.

She hadn't said a word. As crazy as it felt to him, Joe wanted to hear her voice more than he wanted to see her nude at this point. And that was saying a lot, because her body had him in a completely unfamiliar place.

Joe glanced away, though he didn't want to. He looked at the cub. The cub glanced away from his meal to his mother, then noticed she'd changed. He murmured a low growl, a rumbling of uncertainty, then stood on two legs, still in bear cub form.

The cub roared a cry that sounded more scared than anything else and ran for his human mother. As soon as he'd reached her, he ran his nose over her as if confused.

Out of the corner of his eye, Joe saw her kneel and

take the baby in her arms. He kept his gaze averted, studying the horizon over the treetops, enjoying the view of the mountains his family had called home for generations. He listened to the soft cooing the woman made to the little bear. Her tender sounds blended with the creek's gurgling. The little one began to make blowing noises that Joe realized quickly were the sounds of snoring.

"Why do you not have clothing? Does your clothing not shift with you?" Joe kept his voice low, knowing that the woman's bear hearing would enable her to hear what a human couldn't.

He turned to look at her, but kept his eyes on her face. Not that he could see anything of that remarkably sexy body even if he wanted to, the way she was huddled, sitting cross-legged on the forest floor, pine needles serving as a cushion and the baby bear covering her nudity.

Was she not going to talk to him? Then a peculiar thought hit him. Maybe she couldn't talk? In this day and age, how could a shifter not speak in a human language? Impossible. She had to speak.

"If you're not going to talk to me, maybe you could just let me get down and go on my way?" He tried one last time, though he had no plan to get down from the tree without her permission.

He wasn't sure if she could kill him. Though as a bear

she was large and fearsome, Joe had grown up with bear shifters. He could hold his own, even barehanded.

He rubbed his jaw, his unshaven growth making scratchy sounds in the otherwise quiet forest.

"Stay."

She spoke! She could communicate.

Elation coursed through his body, replacing lust. He'd been worried otherwise.

He needed clarification regarding her statement, though. "Stay in the tree? Or stay in the area?"

She cocked her head, the same way her bear had. "Stay in the tree, for now."

"Do you have a name?" He thought that was a valid question, considering she was pretty much feral.

"Doesn't everyone?" Her full lips, red tinged, curled into the slightest smile, as though she found an internal joke amusing.

"Care to share it with me? Does he have a name?" Joe pointed to the sleeping cub.

"Thank you for the food," she said.

"Are you staying long? Where are you traveling to?"

"Traveling to? Why couldn't we just stay here?"

"You're in Bear Canyon Valley territory. You're trespassing. You don't have permission to be here."

"Who owns this property?" She stroked the baby bear's fur backward.

"The U.S. government."

"Then I don't see how I need permission to be on public property."

"Shifter code. You know how that is."

"What?" Genuine confusion passed over her features.

The branch dug into his ass uncomfortably. He wasn't a kid anymore. He couldn't perch in trees indefinitely, and he found himself a little impatient. "Every shifter knows shifter code. This is Forester territory."

It had been when Brad Forester, Mae's bear shifter mate had been around. Grant was the alpha now, but they'd never started calling it Waters territory. That just seemed wrong and disrespectful to Brad, a man whom everyone had looked up to, including Joe's long gone great-great-grandfather. Oral history among Joe's people referred to the shifter battle during which Brad had died.

"Should that mean something to me?" Her voice wasn't hostile, but it wasn't awed or afraid, either.

Could someone really live in a vacuum? What shifter family out there wasn't aware of territories and trespassing? Or maybe she was aware and didn't give a damn.

"Shifters don't live long if they ignore territorial boundaries," Joe told her.

"I can take care of myself and..." She pointed to the little one. "...him."

"What's his name?"

"You seem stuck on names. What's yours?" She

quirked a brow, her gaze intelligent and bold, challenging too.

"Joe Dark."

"What kind of name is that?"

"It would be Joe Dark Eagle Rises After Winter Storm except that my family shortened it." He allowed a small smile. "Thank the Great Spirit."

"You're Native American."

"Part," he admitted. "Most, actually. That bothers you?"

"No. I've heard that your people are in tune with people and animals. Is that how you knew what I am?"

"No. I live with shifters. Grew up with them. Just knew."

Not totally true. Joe had a second sense. He wondered if it had anything to do with Mae being a distant cousin. Mae had powers too, it had been said when Joe was younger. He'd heard stories of Mae, even though she'd left the valley for a while after Brad had died, and it took a long time for her to return. She'd returned before Joe was born, and she never changed, never really aged.

"It's the shifter's couple bonding," Joe's grandmother used to say. "It gives shifters' mates powers." Then his grandmother would shake her head and add, "As if Mae needed more powers."

Joe never really knew. He and Mae, for all their distant relationship, weren't as close as Grant and Mae had been over the years. Maybe because Joe chose to leave the valley too, for a while. First the military, then he'd chased the rodeo across the country, performing and avoiding Bear Canyon Valley.

When Joe's grandfather died, his grandmother had said Joe needed to come back, that the Waters family would need him the way they'd needed his grandfather. A human guardian.

"So now what, Joe Dark?" She studied him, unmoving, unflinching, unyielding.

"You let me help you."

She laughed, an unpleasant sound that spilled distrust.

He didn't care for the sound. He knew it wasn't an example of her true nature.

"Why does it surprise you that I would want to help you?"

"What is it that you will help me with, Joe Dark?"

He found himself in a quandary about the way she said his name. Part of him liked it, liked her. The other part of him made him feel mocked.

"If you won't let me help you, I suggest you leave the territory. It will not bode well for you to be here. The shifters who live here don't tolerate trespassers. They don't want to see any of their kind harmed by trespassers, rovers, or rivals."

"How many shifters are there here in this territory?"

Screw this. Joe wasn't going to give her any information if she didn't give him any. He crossed his arms.

God, but his ass was getting numb from the damned branch. "I need to get down. Should I be concerned about an attack?"

She shrugged an elegant café-au-lait-colored shoulder. "Should I?"

"Have I tried to attack you? I've brought food to you and the little one, and never tried to attack or approach."

Her eyes closed to slits. "Could be you're the long plan type."

"Tell you what." He fought to keep his temper in check, but knew it wasn't solely anger with her that was bubbling to the surface. "Why don't you take him and go. Then I'll just go my own way."

Of course, he had no clue what he'd tell the shifters of Bear Canyon Valley about this statement, but he'd deal with it later.

Right now he needed to get away from this woman. She'd already given him a raging hard-on. Now she was making her way into his emotions, with her feisty attitude and fiercely bold independence.

He didn't need emotions. He needed her to get the hell away from him.

Little one still in her arms, she rose, turned on her heel, and walked away, toward the forest.

Her body was a lush testament to her womanhood,

that ass swaying in just the right way, tempting and teasing him with the curves and sashaying.

A few more long paces, and she was gone, as if she'd never been there.

And she didn't even eat. He shook his head and adjusted his pants. His cock ached from pressing against denim for so long. It ached from years of not having a woman. He allowed his palm to drag across it with a long, hard, deliberate stroke, that beautiful, strong woman on his mind.

CHAPTER THREE

Kane and Astra had invited Joe, Kelsey, and Teague over. They'd also invited Tanner and Marti, but Marti had begged off because little Dominic, Marti's toddler shifter son, had the sniffles. Teague's truck was already in the driveway, parked next to Kane's vehicle. Kelsey and Teague were here.

Joe pulled up and parked his truck. Kane and Astra had a place that was remote, just like Kane liked, as far away as possible from civilization. Kane struggled with his bear and Astra had mentioned that being so far from town allowed him to go out to the woods and be alone with his bear. Joe didn't understand it, but then again, he wasn't a shifter, so he didn't need to.

Joe exhaled, but it wasn't a sigh of relief. More like a sigh of trepidation. He knew they were going to ask about the female shifter, and he didn't want to share her with them. He didn't want to share anything about her with anyone yet. He wondered about his selfishness and possessiveness for her.

He shoved that aside. He didn't need to have thoughts about her, about what she stirred up in him. Damn it. He'd failed. He should have gotten some answers for them. The shifters of Bear Canyon Valley had every right to be concerned about strange or trespassing shifters. They didn't understand that she wasn't a threat. He could see it in her. She was a loner. She had no allies to bring forward to hurt the valley's shifters.

The two couples were on the porch, visiting and enjoying iced tea and ice-cold beers. Joe shoved his hands through his hair—way too long, he knew—but who had time for a haircut these days?

Fifteen minutes and some small talk—it didn't take long for them to bring it up. Kelsey of course was first, as she was the one who had actually held the cub. Teague had shared with all of them how that had impacted her. It was no secret she'd miscarried Teague's baby a couple years back and had suffered from that for a long time.

"Did you see her?" Kelsey's eyes bored into Joe's, eager for answers. "Did you see the baby? Is it okay?"

"It's fine." Joe took a swig of the beer, hoping that answer would suffice. He should have known better.

"What does she want?" Astra's tone was nervous.

Astra's mother had been killed right here in Bear Canyon Valley while Joe was away on the rodeo circuit.

He hadn't known the Evans family: Doc, his wife, and Astra, her daughter from another marriage.

Trespassing shifters had killed Astra's mother. Astra had remained untrusting of almost all shifters for a long time, and Doc Evans had taken his stepdaughter away and raised her in Florida.

Joe hadn't really gotten to know them until after they'd returned.

Everyone had been surprised when Doc and Astra returned to Bear Canyon Valley, but it seemed fated, as none of them could imagine a life in the valley without Doc and Astra. And now that Astra had found happiness and love with a shifter, she'd gotten over her animosity for shifters, it seemed. Except she still harbored a natural suspiciousness about shifters who didn't belong and might be dangerous to the Bear Canyon Valley clan.

Kelsey looked at Astra. Astra shrugged. Kelsey turned back to Joe. "And?"

He took his time putting the beer bottle down, studying the label, deliberating his answer. "She's not here to hurt anyone. She's..." He chewed on the thought some more. "She's just here. For now. Needed a place for a bit." He wasn't lying. Not technically, though of course she hadn't told him all that. Not in so many words. Not in any words.

"What's her name?" Astra turned those eerie green gorgeous eyes on him. Joe was reminded of a luminescent green crystal ball every time he looked into her eyes.

Joe knew about her gift of seeing shifters. Humans didn't typically have that skill. Joe suspected she had more unexpected and undiscovered skills, but it wasn't his place to go poking around in anyone else's business. Whatever skills Astra had, she'd find them in her own good time. And if she didn't find them, Mae would see to it that she did. Joe knew how Mae operated.

Mae. Joe pushed that thought away. Mae and Doc had left town for Dallas for a couple days. With Grant gone on his honeymoon and Mae and Doc out of town, there wasn't really an alpha here. If something came up before any of them returned, who'd be the decision-maker?

"Joe? Her name?" Astra prompted him again, her eyes aglow.

"Don't know."

Kane clapped him on the back. "You okay?"

"Just got a lot on my mind," Joe said. *Like a stunning, ebony-haired, mocha-skinned beauty with a handful of a cub on her hands and an air of independence.* Not only did she have that air of independence, she had something else. She reminded Joe of a mountain lion he'd seen once, a wounded one who didn't trust anyone or anything.

CHAPTER FOUR

Another try. After dinner the other night, Joe had come back every day. And every day he'd brought something different for them to eat.

He'd also brought something else, something he'd brought back from the city. Christ, he hated driving into the city. Hated the concrete, the glass, the smell. He'd had enough of cities. Cities brought back images of bomb-destroyed buildings. These days he found his pleasure in the forest, typically alone. Why did he drive into the city? For clothing for the woman. He'd estimated her size as best as he could and had been getting ready to pay when he thought of the little tyke.

Going back to the children's section, he'd picked out various clothing sizes of jeans and t-shirts and a jacket. He picked up several sizes of shoes for both the little bear and the woman.

It had been four days since he'd brought the clothing, four days of bringing food and waiting. Joe no longer climbed the tree anymore. He waited by a large boulder, sometimes sitting on it, for hours, waiting. She'd come, he knew, but it must have been after he left.

She's not coming until after dark, after I'm long gone.

This wasn't going to work. Her arriving after he was long gone wasn't going to provide a resolution for the Bear Canyon Valley shifters. At least not one that would end well for her.

He'd bet she could hear him, though. He'd wager she wasn't too far out of hearing range—bear hearing range. Much better than his.

"I know you're around. You need to learn how to trust someone, sooner or later. And by damn, I haven't given you cause not to trust me yet."

"Have you given me cause to trust you?" Her voice came from close by. Very close by.

Joe didn't turn abruptly, though he wanted to. He was lying on the boulder, eyes closed. He rose to a sitting position slowly.

She was in front of him.

He smiled. "You're a whole different being, aren't you?"

She was wearing one of the dresses he'd gotten for her. It was a bit snug, but in all the good ways and in all the right places. She was in her human form, but the little one was a bear, waiting by a tree, eyes curious and unafraid.

"Ivan. You can eat," she told the cub.

"Nice name." Joe tried to be casual about his exuberance over learning the cub's name.

"Ivan the Terrible. It fits him." She smiled.

He made a conscious effort to close his mouth, which had dropped open. When she smiled, her visage turned from one of closed intensity to openness. Her full lips curved into a cupid's bow that showed perfect white teeth.

"He's not that terrible," Joe countered, to keep it light, though he couldn't stop staring at her. "I've seen a bit of him. I'd say he's typical for his age."

"I'd say he's a rascal who keeps me on my toes and from getting any rest. He wanders off, he's loud when he should be quiet, and he's awake when he should be asleep."

"Sounds like an average little boy to me. But I guess it must be rough, being a single mom and all."

Her face turned somber. "I never said I was a single mom."

"You have been while you've been in this forest, so..." He paused. "I guess I assumed."

She nodded. "Sara."

He froze. What the hell. What had changed her mind? "Nice to meet you, Sara."

He held his hand out. She put her hand in his. Her

touch was hot, creating a rush that traveled throughout his body. He found every pore and nerve ending in his being responding to that touch. He tried to fight the sensation, to get it to go away, but yet, it persisted.

How could such a small hand turn into that bear? He wanted to shake it then release it, but he found himself holding it for a second too long. Maybe many seconds too long.

A confused expression passed over her face, and her dark eyes glowed with a yellow flame for a moment.

Her bear was surfacing. Would she shift right now?

CHAPTER FIVE

Sara recoiled from the touch. She wanted to pull away from the intensity of the jolt that had passed through her when her hand had touched his. She'd never felt anything like that before.

The other half of her wanted to recoil and pull away from him because she had nothing but hatred for humans.

Her bear rumbled in her mind, wanting the man called Joe Dark.

Dark Eagle Rises After Winter Storm, he'd said his name was. She found that easy enough to believe. He was a dark eagle, with that long black hair of his that cascaded in a shiny sheet and touched his shoulders. Some days, he wore it in a ponytail.

She fought the urge to touch her own tangled, unruly

mess from living without a brush for so long. Finger-combing just didn't cut it.

She looked at his face, the profile, that nose that was an eagle's beak yet aquiline and strong. High cheekbones, full lower lip that broke the severe austerity of his less generous upper lip. His own eyes were dark, though not as dark as hers, she knew.

She didn't allow her gaze the luxury of traveling down his body again. She'd already noticed his chest, shoulders, and arms that were thicker than tree branches.

She pushed back the blush that threatened to kiss her cheeks with color when she thought of the way he'd looked at her body when she'd shifted that first time.

Her bear had scented his arousal and responded, as had Sara's body. Her core had become moist and flexed for him. Her breasts had ached for his touch, and her nipples had puckered. How could a man she'd never met—well, not really met—have this effect on her?

How can I want him when I don't even know him?

Her bear rose to the occasion, an answer at the ready. She pushed her bear back. She'd heard this argument before, when Joe had been here. She'd heard it several times before from her bear. Over and over.

You can't know he's supposed to be ours, Sara countered. *That's not how it works.*

Her bear roared in her mind.

Of course I don't know how it works. How could I? I can't

believe this would be how it works. How can you know so soon?

Her bear was quick to remind her who had saved them. Her bear had taken her from that place; it had brought her here. It had protected and fed her and Ivan.

Sara fought the temptation of him while her bear embraced it. As much as Sara fought it, she only half did so, for another part of her was impossibly and irreversibly drawn to this man who'd brought them food and clothing, and then had waited patiently.

"Nice to meet you, too." She managed to get the words out though her mind felt like it was mush.

"Tell me about yourself." His voice rolled over her, soothing like the warmest breeze in the spring right after the cold winter nights.

I can't. "Not much to tell."

He gave her a look. He didn't buy it. At all.

Ivan noticed her talking to him. He'd never seen her talking to another person before. He'd never seen her shift into her human form as much as he had recently.

"How does he like his clothes?" Joe asked.

He's never worn human clothes. "I haven't put them on him yet." Trying to keep secrets from Joe was becoming difficult. If she wasn't lying, she was evading, at the very least.

It's not like I owe him the truth. Or anything at all. Yet, she felt like she did owe him. She wanted to tell him everything. She wished she could tell him the whole story, but that was something she'd never done. Ever.

"Will you ever trust me?" He still held her hand in his, not tightly, but gently, giving her the option to remove hers. Something she didn't want to do.

I doubt I'll be here long enough. "I do trust you. Some." She would need to leave as soon as possible. This short conversation, the way he'd looked at her the other day, the way he was looking at her now, the impact of his touch on her...

She absolutely had to get far away from him before she did something she would regret.

"You know if you need anything—" he started to say.

"I know where you live. That cabin, not far from the big house."

His brow rose, but a smile appeared on his face. "You followed me?" His smile grew. "It's not easy to get the jump on me, but you seem to have done it a couple of times."

Her cheeks grew warm. She'd been caught. Yes, she'd followed him and she wouldn't lie to herself by pretending that it had just been to make sure he wasn't a threat. She couldn't lie to herself, anyway; her bear wouldn't let her get away with it.

She turned her glance toward the west and looked over the trees to the mountains beyond. That was the direction she'd take Ivan next. Perhaps California. It was a large state, so they could merge into the population there and go unnoticed. And there was a lot of land, plenty of state parks.

She grew sad at the idea of leaving this beautiful valley. Sad at the idea of leaving Joe behind.

Across from her, by the food, Ivan snuffled and lifted his head. He was full. He'd be wanting his nap next. If she held Ivan while he slept, then she'd be stuck talking to Joe.

The idea wasn't bad. She'd enjoy getting to know him better, but she feared he'd spend his time trying to find out more about her than talking about himself.

"I should go. It's time for his nap."

Joe tightened his grip on her hand. "Can I meet him?"

"No." She hadn't meant to say it with such vehemence.

He rose, pulled her up. "If you need anything…" Joe let go of her hand once she was on her feet. "I'd like to visit with you again. Say, tomorrow? Do you have any favorites?"

She fought the urge to laugh and ask him if he thought that these were dates. She knew the answer already. She could see emotions in his eyes. Her bear could smell his emotions. Sara understood her bear's feelings for Joe too well; she felt many of those same feelings.

If she were smart, she'd be gone tomorrow. "You choose," she told him, and felt horrible for being a liar.

CHAPTER SIX

Joe shouldered the backpack he'd filled with a few toiletries. He wasn't sure they'd be what she'd want, but he'd noticed the way she'd touched her hair self-consciously. He didn't want to tell her he liked her hair, liked the whole just-got-fucked look of her hair.

Yeah, that probably wouldn't go over too well.

God knew, he wanted to take that woman and do things with her and to her that hadn't crossed his mind in a long time. What the hell. He'd gone from being a man immune to sex to a man who walked around with a raging hard-on all the time.

He'd picked up a chocolate cake, too. For Ivan. He'd yet to see the little boy in his human skin, and he looked forward to seeing him that way. He intended to ask Sara to let him shift. Why hadn't the little one shifted yet?

Joe put the food by the usual tree and took his spot at

the boulder that had been a silent sentinel, witnessing his meetings with Sara. Setting the backpack down, he relaxed. He hadn't been able to sleep since he'd met Sara. Every night he wondered if she and the little cub were okay.

He closed his eyes, confident his senses would let him know when she'd arrived.

A SHIVER COURSED THROUGH JOE, WAKING HIM UP. HE bolted upright. It was getting dark and a chill was settling into the air. Where the hell was Sara? He ran to the food.

Untouched. He looked for foot and paw prints around the food, but found no fresh tracks at all. Where the hell was she?

"Sara," he called out softly, knowing she didn't like Ivan upset and Ivan seemed sensitive to human voices.

No response.

He called her name again.

Again, nothing.

He deliberated calling Ivan's name. That seemed like a lowdown thing to do, using the kid to pull the mother out. But maybe it wasn't lowdown. Maybe she'd forgotten. Or was busy.

"Ivan." He didn't yell it out. There was no reason to do that; the little bear shifter would hear him.

He heard a sound. A whimper. Would that be Ivan? Surely not, because that meant Sara would be nearby, and she wouldn't ignore him. Would she?

Maybe she would. She seemed reluctant to engage with him at times. She definitely was extremely secretive.

Still. Joe couldn't leave the forest without checking on that whimper.

He stepped away from the boulder, walking toward the area he'd heard the whimper come from.

"Ivan." He whispered the little one's name. "You're not playing hide and seek, are you?"

That would be very unlike the little bear. He'd had no interaction with Joe. If anything, he'd seemed wary, as if unsure of him—men—maybe humans in general, judging from the way he'd looked at his mother when she'd shifted the first couple times.

Why would he not be familiar with humans?

Joe walked softly, but not too softly. He didn't want to sneak up on Sara, especially not if she was in bear form. For sure she could inflict a world of hurt on him, and he wouldn't want to hurt her in return, not even while he was defending himself.

He heard the whimpering noise again. He was definitely headed in the right direction. He looked back at the horizon to the west. It would be dark soon.

He almost tripped over something. A yelp told him what it was.

"Hell. I'm sorry, Ivan." He knelt next to the shifter cub and put his hand out.

Ivan pulled back a little, his eyes round and scared.

"What's wrong, little fella? Where's your mom?" He kept his hand out.

Ivan sniffed toward him.

"It's me, Joe. Your mom's friend. Remember?"

Ivan came closer. Joe put his hand on Ivan's shoulder and ran it over his back.

The cub was wet. Had he just been swimming? Was that where Sara was? Joe looked at his hand. His palm was dark.

Blood? Blood!

"Are you hurt?" He ran his fingers over Ivan gently, looking for injury. "Where's your mother?"

If Sara wasn't with Ivan... Oh, fuck. Joe didn't care for where his mind was going, but it seemed like the only logical explanation.

"Ivan."

The cub looked at him, pain and a question in his eyes.

"I need you to take me to your mom. Take me to Sara, right now."

Ivan glanced toward the forest, then back at Joe.

"Now, before it gets dark." *Before she dies, if she's hurt.*

A devastating pain rendered Joe's heart in two. He couldn't breathe. His lungs burned with the air he couldn't release at the thought of Sara being dead.

Mother Nature, Great Spirit, Christ—he'd pray to all of them though he wasn't sure what he believed in at this stage of his life. He'd pray to everything and anything that she wasn't dead. He'd make a deal with the devil himself to keep her alive.

What if she were already dead? Who would take care of Ivan? The valley would. One of the shifter families would take him in. No, he wasn't going to think that way. He wasn't going to let that happen.

Ivan began to walk toward the forest, picking up his pace with every step he took, shortly turning it into a run, as fast as his little legs could carry him.

Joe followed, trying to stay far enough behind that Ivan wouldn't get spooked by being chased.

Thirty yards into their run, Ivan came to an abrupt stop.

There she was. In human form. Prone, huddled in a near-fetal position, her legs splayed somewhat. She was wearing the dress he'd bought for her.

"Sara?" Joe called her name softly. He was still a few yards away. He walked at a brisk pace, approaching her and Ivan who was huddle next to her, his dark eyes focused on Joe's approach.

She didn't answer. She didn't stir.

Fear grabbed Joe's heart and twisted it, then shoved it upward until it felt like it was trapped in his throat.

Ivan let out a low roar, an odd sound coming from

such a young shifter cub. He used his paws on his mother's legs, pushing and pulling on them.

Joe froze when he saw something sticking out of her back. No, two somethings.

Fuck. Arrows. Hunters? Here? Were they a threat to Ivan or Sara? She'd gone into her human form, not by choice. She was unconscious.

Joe reached for her neck, put a finger over her pulse point. It beat, but weakly. The air around them was heavy with the scent of her blood.

He pushed the hair away from her face. Definitely not conscious.

He looked over her body to see if there were more arrows.

None.

"We need to get her to a doctor." How the hell was he going to carry her and Ivan? Would Ivan follow? Would Ivan shift for him?

He put his hand on the little bear's shoulder. "Can you shift?"

The bear cub grunted, then snorted. And nothing.

Shit.

Joe took out his phone and pressed the third button on speed dial. The phone had barely been answered before Joe began to talk.

"Doc, I have an emergency." How the hell could he get Doc here? He couldn't give him directions. Damn. "Get your kit and meet me at my place. Bring Astra too."

He hung up and shoved his phone back in his pocket. He should have told them to bring more help, in case Ivan needed something, in case Sara shifted and became belligerent.

How the hell was he going to get Sara to his place, a good twenty-minute walk at least? And would Ivan follow? Or would he try to stop Joe, thinking he was protecting his mother?

Joe cleared his throat. He wasn't sure he could talk. He was overwhelmed with emotions. He had to talk, he needed to get Ivan to follow him home. He couldn't leave Ivan here. If he did and something happened to Ivan...

He shook his head. He didn't want to think about that.

"Ivan." He put his hand on Ivan's shoulder. This would be much easier if he were in human form, if only to make Joe feel like he was talking to someone who would understand him. "I need to help your mom. You know we're friends. I have to take her to my place. A doctor will meet us there and make her beater. You have to trust me."

Ivan growled. He stepped back, then stepped between Joe and Sara.

"Son, look. I know she's your mom. I know you want to protect her. Right now the only chance she has is to let Doc see to her. You have got to understand that. Now let me help her."

Ivan showed Joe his teeth, stood on two legs, roared his helplessness.

Joe fought back the emotions. His heart ached, going out to the little one. The young cub must be confused by all that was happening.

"Let me help her. I swear I will." Joe knelt in front of the cub, looked him in the eye. "You know I would never hurt her. Ever."

Ivan grunted.

The first thing I'm going to do when Sara gets better is ask her why the hell he doesn't shift.

Communication would have been a whole lot easier if Ivan could shift into human form.

Joe put one arm under her legs and one under her torso, careful not to come near the protruding arrows, and lifted her up. Her dress was red, soaked with her blood. He clenched his jaw in anger. He'd find out who did this. He'd find out, and there'd be hell to pay. He'd call the park rangers to find out if any poachers or illegal hunters had been spotted in the area.

"Let's go, Ivan."

The little cub followed him without incident. Either he understood what was going on or he trusted Joe, because he stayed on Joe's heels, making soft sounds that broke Joe's heart. If he hadn't had to carry Sara, he'd have picked up little Ivan to comfort him.

CHAPTER SEVEN

Doc's truck was already at Joe's cabin when he and Ivan walked up, with a still unconscious Sara in Joe's arms.

Doc and Astra were pacing the porch, and Kane was sitting on the rail.

"What the hell...?" Kane muttered when he saw Joe walk up.

Ivan stopped short in his tracks. He rose up on two legs and roared at Kane. It was a sight and sound that would have made Joe laugh on a normal day, the little pint-sized cub threatening a full-grown shifter. Especially a shifter like Kane, who was no small being.

"Ivan. No. They're friends." Joe tried to calm him as Doc and Astra stared from the porch steps. "Can you get the door?" Joe asked.

Doc flung the door open and stepped aside.

"This is the one you were talking about, isn't it?" Astra pointed to Sara. "The shifter from the forest?"

Joe knew about Astra's gift. She could sight a shifter immediately—it had something to do with their aura. "Yeah."

Kane looked at Ivan. "Why isn't he... why's he in his bear?"

Joe shook his head. "I'm not sure he knows how to shift."

"What?" Doc and Kane's voices were shocked and simultaneous.

"How can he not know how to shift?" Kane stood back while Joe walked into the cabin with Sara.

Joe stepped over the threshold, then turned to Ivan. "Come in."

Ivan looked from one to the other, then stepped back with a small grunt.

"Look," Joe began, "if you're not there when your mom wakes up, she'll be frantic. We can't have that happening. It wouldn't be good for her. Now come on." He turned his back on Ivan and walked toward his guest bedroom. Doc was already in there, and Astra followed Joe.

Joe let out a sigh of relief when he heard Ivan's claws clicking on the cabin's wood floor. He laid Sara out on the bed, close to the same position he'd found her in.

"Who the fuck would do that?" Kane's voice was gruff with anger.

Joe looked for Ivan. He wasn't in the room, so Joe poked his head out the door and saw the cub in the hallway between the guest bedroom and the entrance.

"You can come here, if you want, and keep an eye on your mom."

Ivan didn't move.

Joe knelt and held his arms out.

Ivan scampered toward him at a run. The force of his leap into Joe's arms almost knocked him over. He regained his balance and stood, hugging the cub like a baby, his hand on Ivan's head.

Astra came close. "Hi, Ivan. I'm Astra."

Ivan made a grumbling sound.

"Doc's my dad. He's a special doctor. He's great with shifters. That's what your mom is. That's what you are."

Ivan snorted, blowing hot air out of his nostrils. The breath warmed Joe's shoulder while he watched Doc cut the fabric of the dress Joe had bought for Sara. The fabric, once a beautiful, flowing yellow with tiny white flowers, was now a rusty, reddish color. It fell away from Sara's light brown skin, dropping to the floor, revealing her bloodstained flesh.

Joe kept his hand on the back of Ivan's head, keeping him from moving so he wouldn't see his mother like that.

Kane walked up behind them. "He needs to learn how to shift as soon as possible. It could save his life. It may have saved his mother's life. I'd bet she was in her bear when this happened."

Joe didn't want to tell Kane that Sara spent most of her time in her bear. "Don't know if he'll come to you."

"I know who he would go to," Kane said.

Kelsey stepped out from behind him. "Hi, baby bear," she said. Her voice had a tinge of sadness in it. "Remember me?"

Ivan raised his head quickly and looked behind Joe. He squirmed slightly in Joe's arms. Joe wondered if the little bear would consider going to her.

Kelsey continued talking. "Of course you remember me. I fed you that bar, in the cave, that tunnel." She held her hand up. "I have another one if you want it."

Ivan looked at his mother.

"I'll be here with her." Joe scratched Ivan behind the ears. "I won't leave her or let anything happen to her. Go with Kelsey. You'll still be nearby. I'll call you if she wakes up."

"Come on." Teague appeared from behind Kelsey. "You remember me, too, don't you? Your mom hurt me because she didn't know if we were going to hurt you. We're Joe's friends. You know I could have hurt your mom but I didn't, right?"

Ivan looked from Joe to Teague, then to Kelsey.

"It'll be fine." Kelsey wiggled her fingers for Ivan to come to her.

Joe held him out, leaning toward Kelsey, waiting to see if Ivan would resist.

He didn't. He went to Kelsey's arms without issue,

and she turned and took him into the living room. Kane and Teague followed her. Kane was telling Ivan that he could turn into a human just like he and Teague did. Just like his mom. He was telling him he'd teach him how.

Joe turned his attention back to Doc. Astra was helping Doc, and blocking Joe's view.

Joe went to walk around her but she put her hand on his shoulder. "Doc and I both work better without an audience."

"I don't want to leave her."

Astra studied him with those eerie green eyes that looked like they were lit up from behind. "I can see that she means a lot to you. Just like Ivan had to trust you, you'll have to trust us."

"I'll sit right here, then. I won't say a word or get in the way. Hell, I'll hardly look at you. Just don't ask me to leave." He sucked in a ragged breath. "Please."

Doc looked over his shoulder. "I need you," he said to Astra. "Stay in that chair." Doc indicated a chair with his head, then turned his attention back to Astra. "Gauze and..." Doc shook his head.

Joe fought the urge to jump up and see what he was shaking his head at.

"Got it." Astra looked at what he was doing and began to hand him things.

Joe couldn't see anything they were doing because of the way Astra was standing. Maybe it was better. He couldn't handle watching them dig arrowheads out of Sara's body.

Doc pulled a light blanket over Sara and stepped away from the bed, then turned to Joe. "It's not as bad as it could be," he said. "Just bled a lot. After it's fully staunched and she regains consciousness, she can get into her bear and will heal much faster."

Joe knew all about the fast healing. He prayed she'd gain consciousness quickly so she could shift. The moment she shifted, her healing would be accelerated and she'd begin to go back to normal. With the shifters he knew, recovery from near death could take only a few hours.

He looked at her pale face, her lips no longer the plump, rose-colored lips he'd so enjoyed talking to. The ones he wanted to kiss. To claim.

He gripped the headboard of the sturdy bed with a white-knuckled grasp. The bed had been in his family for decades, crafted long ago by his grandfather.

Doc and Astra stood next to him. Astra put her hand on Joe's hand, as if she got it. Maybe she did. She had those mystical powers, and Joe, like his ancestors before him, believed in mystical powers.

Doc patted Joe's shoulder. "She could have died if you hadn't found her, though," Doc said. "That's a lot of blood loss."

Joe was infused with anger again. He dug his cell out of his pocket called the park rangers and told them he was concerned that there might be poachers with bows and arrows.

The rangers told him they'd picked up a couple of teens and confirmed the brand of arrows. Same ones that had been in Sara.

They asked him if anyone had been hurt. He looked at her, pale, still unconscious.

She'd be furious if he said anything that garnered attention.

"No. Just thought you'd want to know." He gritted his teeth as he lied and thanked them for their time.

CHAPTER EIGHT

Sara groaned. She tried to stretch. God, there was a horrible sting and a throbbing ache in her shoulder. And back. And even her chest.

Then she noticed the softness beneath her. It was a mattress. It took a second for that to sink in. Then she noticed the smell—that was not the forest smell, it was an indoor smell.

Was she back at Crossroads? The horror of being back there felt like a million piranhas were feasting on her gut. Her eyes flew open.

The place she was in was unfamiliar, but it wasn't Crossroads. Where was Ivan? She tried to sit up. Grunted from the pain, but managed.

"Hey," a voice said softly.

She knew that voice.

Joe.

Sara turned her head. He was sitting in a chair, watching her.

"Ivan." That was all she could manage with a dry mouth and a knotted stomach.

Then she noticed something—no, someone—in his arms. A dark brown mop of curly hair. Clearly asleep.

"Ivan?" Where was her son? She looked at Joe for answers.

"Kane and Teague taught him how to shift."

"That's too dangerous." She palmed the mattress and tried to push herself up again. "You don't understand. If they find out I had him... At his age..."

Tears sprang to her eyes. She couldn't see Joe or Ivan clearly anymore; they were swimming in her tears.

Joe rose to his feet. "Have you ever thought how dangerous it could be for him that he can't shift?"

"I know how dangerous it is. I've spent years knowing how dangerous it is. I do not want him around humans. I do not want him to be a part of his human side." She fisted the light blanket covering her, then pushed it away.

What the hell?

She wasn't dressed. "Where are my clothes?" She yanked the blanket back up.

Joe stepped closer to the bed. "He's had dinner. Want me to lay him next to you on the bed? We need to talk."

Sara moved over so that Ivan could lie next to her. She brushed a kiss against his forehead. The bandages pulled as she stretched the skin attached to them. A sting and an ache made her wonder if she had stitches.

"Who took care of me? Where am I?"

"You're in my cabin. Doc did. You're among your kind here. And safe. And Ivan is safe." He pulled the chair close to the bed.

CHAPTER NINE

Joe appraised her. She was pale, because of the blood loss, he was sure. Her eyes had dark circles beneath them and she had an overall haggard look to her.

The way she pulled the blanket up to cover her body was very different from the confident woman who'd stood there, fully naked, proud, hands on her hips, defying him.

What was Crossroads? Why was it more dangerous for Ivan to be human than a bear?

Her head cocked as if she were listening to something. "Who's out there?"

"My friends."

"Shifters or humans?"

"Both." He scrubbed at his face, pushed his hair back over his shoulder. "Three shifters and two of their human mates. One is the shifter who took care of you, Doc. He's a doctor who specializes in shifters. Two other shifters taught Ivan how to shift. And Astra, Doc's daughter. And Kelsey." Joe paused. "She's the one who found Ivan in the cave, I guess."

Understanding dawned on her face. "I see."

"Why are you so hell-bent on his staying a bear?"

"It's safer for him that way."

"Safer from what?"

She sighed, looked away, at a picture on the wall. "Is that you?"

Joe didn't need to look to answer. It was a picture of him and his grandfather, the last one taken of them together. "Yup. Me and Old One."

"Old One?"

"What we called my grandfather."

"Family." The word came out as if each syllable was ripped from her past and her soul. "I can't stay here. I need to go."

"Listen, Sara. You're weak. What you need to do to recuperate is shift into your bear and rest. You'll be fine in a few hours if you do that. If you don't, you'll take longer to heal."

"I can just shift into my bear and go. I'll heal while I travel." Her tone was despondent.

The words and her tone made Joe sad. "What the hell are you running from?" He stood up too quickly.

She put her arms around Ivan protectively.

"I would never do anything to hurt either of you. Don't you know that yet?"

He saw the tension leave her shoulders. Her face became paler, her expression strained.

"You need to recuperate. Please, shift. Keep Ivan with you if it makes you feel better. He can shift by himself when he wakes up. Sleep. I'll be here. I'll watch over you."

The face he'd already fallen for became a little more relaxed. The line her full lips had thinned to left, and she became something closer to the old Sara. The Sara he'd spent weeks watching.

She nodded, cautiously.

"When you wake up, we'll talk."

Sara cocked her head at him.

"I mean it. You're not running out on me until we've talked." He stood in the doorway. "That bed will hold a full-grown bear. It has before. My grandfather built it. Shift and hold him. If he or you call for me, I'll be right outside this door."

He pulled the door closed behind him.

CHAPTER TEN

A hand on his shoulder woke Joe. He looked up. Kane.

"Anything?" Kane asked.

Joe shook his head. "Not a sound." He kept his voice low so that he wouldn't wake her up.

"Seems the little one would be getting hungry at some point, though he ate a ton before he fell asleep."

"I hope she's doing better." Joe rubbed his sleepy eyes.

"She probably is. I heard the window open earlier. Probably got some fresh air."

Joe bounced out of his chair. "Aw, damn." She could have slipped out and could be in another county by now. "How long was I asleep?" He reached for the door handle. "Locked." It had to be locked from the inside. He reared back to shoulder it open.

"Whoa." Kane put his arm across the door, blocking him. "Don't you think you should knock before you bust it open?"

Joe took a deep breath. Kane didn't know her. Then again, Joe wondered, *What makes me think she'd have slipped out the window?*

"Okay." He knocked on the door, lightly.

Nothing.

"See?" he hissed at Kane. "Now move."

He reared back again and a hair's breadth before his shoulder hit the door, he was propelled through the doorway and reaching for purchase to keep from diving headlong into the wall across the rom.

Sara stood by the door she'd opened just before he could crash into it, the blanket wrapped around her, a curious look on her face. "What are you doing?"

"I... I was making sure you're okay." Joe stumbled through the sentence. "I didn't hear any response to my knock."

"I needed a second to shift and open the door."

"Mama?" Ivan sat up, his long hair in his face. He was in one of Joe's spare t-shirts since all the clothing Joe had bought for him was somewhere in the forest, wherever Sara had put it. The t-shirt hung on him, way too large and way too long, but at least he wasn't naked as a little jaybird, Joe thought.

"I'm right here." Sara turned toward him. "I'll get you something, just a moment."

Joe drank in the sight of her. God, she was getting better, returning to the firebrand she'd been before. Her cheeks had a little bit of color in them, probably anger with him for busting in on her like that. It was evident that he didn't trust her, he was sure. How could he convince her it was motivated by how much he cared for her?

Her full lips weren't pale pink anymore. They'd reverted to the rosebuds he wanted to kiss. He tried to look away from her lips, but damn if his tongue and his cock didn't rule the way he was thinking. He couldn't pull himself away from the sight of them.

"Joe." She broke him out of his trance.

"Yeah." He raised his gaze to her eyes. Her bear was there, barely kept back by Sara. Her bear shone her amber glory and her love for him.

She felt the same way he did. He wanted to climb to the cabin's rooftop and announce to the universe that he'd found his mate. As he watched, her bear receded, replaced by Sara's hard and unyielding dark gaze.

Joe knew Sara cared for him. Why was she shutting him out this way?

Sara couldn't afford to get close to Joe. Even more importantly, she couldn't afford to let Joe get close to her.

Sara forced her bear back, making her bear submit to her will.

It's for his own good. Do you want Joe hunted and killed? You know they'll kill anyone to take me back to Crossroads.

Her bear snarled. Her bear couldn't argue with that, so she backed off, went back into obscurity, and let Sara do what she had to do to keep herself and Ivan safe, but she let Sara know she was making a mistake. She backed off grumbling and growling, announcing that when she thought the time was right, she'd come back, and it would be her turn to be proven right.

We'll see when that time comes. We'll see.

Behind Joe, Kane said, "I can get Ivan some food."

Before Sara could stop Ivan, he'd scampered from the bed in that t-shirt that was too long for him and looked more like a dress than not, and was heading for the door.

"I'm going with Uncle Kane," Ivan announced with a backward wave and barely a backward glance.

Tears burned at Sara's eyes.

Her baby. The child she'd never had to share with anyone, the child who'd never been anything but a baby bear, was now walking and calling someone with two legs by the name Uncle.

Uncle.

Her little Ivan, who should hate and fear all two-legged creatures, all humans, was now behaving like a little human boy.

She felt a gaze on her and turned her head. Joe was studying her a little too closely. His expression was one of empathy and... what was that?

"Why are you ruining my life?" She couldn't prevent the vehemence that came out. "Why are you doing this?"

Joe reached for her hand took it in his. Electricity passed through her, and she could see that he felt it too. She jerked her hand away from his. Patiently, Joe reached out and took hers again.

"Don't do that. Don't pull away from me until you know."

"Until I know what?" Her voice cracked.

"Until you know what you're walking away from."

I'm walking away from ruining your life and all your shifter friends' lives and maybe even getting you killed. The people who want me would love to have your shifter friends at Crossroads. More fodder for their laboratory.

She didn't know what to say. She couldn't tell him what she knew, and couldn't lie because...

She simply couldn't lie to him. Just couldn't. Not to Joe.

He pulled on her hand. "Let's sit and talk. My friends will take care of Ivan."

The problem was, she knew that they'd take care of him. But could they protect him when they were found? She'd already stayed too long. She'd risked too much. She silently cursed at her bear for insisting they stay. She realized now it was all because of Joe. Her bear couldn't handle leaving, even though Sara had never really talked to him.

Reluctantly she sat. What Joe didn't know—or maybe he did, and that was why he'd barged into the room—was that she had planned on leaving. She'd opened the window, anticipating that she'd want to slip out, then she'd lain back down. She knew that the shifters would have heard the window. They'd have investigated. So she'd lain back down and let things settle, let their suspicions evaporate.

The problem was, she hadn't taken into account that she needed the recuperating rest. She'd sunk into sleep and not woken up until Joe had knocked.

Damn the luck.

And damn that he knew her too well and had anticipated what she planned to do.

She waited for him to talk, her hand still enveloped in the warmth of his large hand. She inhaled his scent, the masculine scent of him imprinting on her senses. She took in the musky scent, and the cinnamon and hickory scent from the ham she was sure he'd smoked and had probably brought to the forest today. She closed her eyes, memorizing the scents so that when she wasn't around him he would be forever in her.

"Who shot you?" His voice was low, intimate.

She opened her eyes, locked her gaze with his, let him have access to her soul and her bear's soul. Her gaze took in his lips, the stubble that was there, that she could hear whenever he touched his face, like he seemed to do when he was thinking or stressed. His high cheekbones, which she'd seen he'd gotten from his grandfather, as well as the long ebony hair that touched large shoulders above a wide chest.

Her breathing synchronized with his. "I don't know. One minute I was walking through the woods, and the next I heard a whistling sound, then another. At about the same moment, I felt the piercing, ice-cold burn of the arrowheads."

His hand squeezed hers, pulling her close. Sara yielded to the tug, her mind and body both surrendering as she leaned into it, and found his body nestled against hers. The wide shoulders were hard with muscles and warm, the worn shirt soft as her cheek rested on his chest. One of his hands was in her hair, holding her firmly in place while the other was around her waist, resting on her hip, his fingertips too close to her ass for comfort.

Desire stirred within her, a desire so fierce, and so neglected that it spun through her body like a tornado.

"It had to be hunters," she said. "Because if it had been anyone else, they wouldn't have just shot and left. They'd have taken me with them."

His thumb was tracing tiny circles on her temple, lulling her into a place of refuge. "Who else could it have been? What is Crossroads?"

She gasped. "How do you know about Crossroads?"

"You said that word while you were unconscious."

She chewed on her lip, bit down on it relentlessly until his thumb landed on it, pressing down and pulling her lip away from her teeth. He left his thumb there, as if it were a kiss from his own lips, as if it were his own tongue. He ran the pad of his thumb over the sensitive flesh of her bottom lip, from one end to the other, then back, slowly, then again.

The sheer sensuality of his thumb taking the intimate journey across her lip made pulses shoot through her body. She felt her core clench, and wished that he didn't elicit so much desire from her. How did he do this?

"Crossroads..." He prompted, moving his thumb away, dropping it to her jawline, where it rested and branded her at the same time.

CHAPTER ELEVEN

Sara exhaled. "It's a place. A bad, bad place."

"Is it a town?" Joe fought to keep his voice level, sure that she could sense what her proximity was doing to him. His nostrils flared as his cock strained against his pants. His body yearned to make her his. Surely she knew what she did to him. Surely her bear knew. It was all he could do to not kiss her, to not claim her as his mate.

His mate? What the hell? When had he started thinking this way? He didn't do what his shifter friends did. Or did he?

How her bear felt was no secret. Was she fighting her bear? Or was something else going on?

"It's a hospital. I guess that's what everyone thinks it is."

"So if that's what people think what it is, but it's not a hospital, what is it?"

"It's hell." Her uttered words were followed by a growl. Her eyes glowed an amber fire, her bear rising up, fury evident. "You have to let me go. Ivan and I can't be found here. It's too risky for you."

"So the solution is to run? Who will protect Ivan if something happens to you?"

Her eyes widened and turned to a molten golden hue, the color of rage. "Nothing can happen to me." A growl underlined her words. "I can't let anything happen to me. He has no one else."

"Something did happen to you and Ivan was unprotected."

Tears welled in her eyes.

"Let me and the rest of the Bear Canyon Valley shifters be your family. Then he'll have someone else, and so will you. You'll have backup."

"You don't understand—"

He interrupted her with his lips on hers. "No. You don't understand," he said against her lips. The fury in her eyes turned to a different kind of flame, a very different type of fire. The amber glow within yielded its spirit to his, giving him what he wanted, but not the flesh he craved.

He lowered his head with the fierceness of a predator, claiming her lips. His kiss was volatile, spurred on by the passions of their mutual attraction, fueled by the danger that threatened her and heightened by their senses, their emotions and the adrenaline of what they'd been through.

His mouth overtook hers. He savored the taste of her while devouring her. Her lips were soft, crushed beneath his, while her tongue succumbed, yielding permission he didn't ask for.

He knew her son and his friends were only a few rooms away. He knew she had something going on that was pulling at her, and pulling her away from him.

They both knew it, but it stopped mattering.

Time tarried.

Emergencies halted.

Danger waited.

The entire universe felt like it had paused and was spinning around them in a holding pattern while he took control of her. His hand twisted in her hair, crushing her lips tighter against his. His other hand swooped under her generous, curvy ass and pulled her closer to him, maneuvering her onto his lap. Her hip was pressed against his throbbing erection.

She wiggled. He groaned, and she drank his groan away with a kiss. Suddenly her aggressiveness became his aggressor's competitor, both wanting control, both needing each other.

Both demanding.

Both yielding.

Neither giving.

He pulled away from her lips, the sensation as destructive and painful as pulling a scab off a large wound.

"You're mine. Say what you want, do what you want, but make no mistake..."

He leaned close, his lips against her parted ones, and he spoke the words into her mouth.

"You. Are. Mine."

She moaned a whispered word.

He could have sworn that whispered word was "yes." But he wasn't willing to take any chances. Not with this independent firebrand.

"Now tell me about Crossroads." He slipped a hand under the blanket, letting it rest just above her knee, but on the inside, where sensitive flesh made his fingertips yearn for more.

"What do you want me to tell you?" Her voice was breathless. Her pulse beat in her neck, visible.

Sexy.

He touched his lips to that telltale pulse, enjoying the rapid beat, the witness it bore to the way she was reacting to him.

What do I want you to tell me? That you want me. That you need me. That you've got to have me in you, with you, around you.

He swallowed that answer back while his fingers traveled upward along her inside thigh, a slow, tortuous inching that made him mad with desire.

She drew a breath in, making a slight whistling sound as it passed over her teeth. Her eyes closed, and the blanket over her breasts swelled with her captive breath.

He could. He knew he could. He could make her his right here, right now. Joe fought back the desire to give in to something that was far more powerful than he.

"Tell me about his place called Crossroads." He placed his lips against her neck, letting the pulse there beat primal against his lips.

She breathed in deeply, against his chest, her body expanding, as if she was preparing herself for battle. He felt the muscles in her legs tighten under his fingertips as she flexed. More preparation for battle?

INSTEAD OF CONTINUING THEIR SINGLE-GOALED PURSUIT, Joe's fingers stopped and waited patiently on her thigh. Sara fought back a sigh. She wanted him as badly as her bear did, but one of them had to be the voice of reason.

Her bear grumbled. *I know, it sucks.*

Sara listened for Ivan's voice. It had a content tone to it. Even happy. He was enjoying his time with the other shifters—and humans. Damn Joe for doing this, a part of her thought. The other part of her rejoiced that Ivan had something he'd never had before.

She looked at the man whose lap she sat in. She

knew there was a question on the table, and she knew he was waiting patiently for an answer to that question. She studied his features. He wasn't thickly built like his shifter friends, but he lacked no muscle, lacked no definition. Half the time, his hair had been pulled into a ponytail, the other half it flowed loose, reminding her of his Native American heritage.

His full bottom lip under the more spare upper one, his high cheekbones, the intensity of his dark gaze. She swallowed her desire back, though her body pulsed for him. Her channel was flexing and clenching, needing him as she'd never needed a man before.

"Sara." That one word, her name, as it passed over his lips was a blessing, a curse, an order, a demand, and a plea. "I'm waiting," he hissed.

He adjusted slightly, a reminder of the length of hardness that was pressing against her hip—making no demands, but taking her prisoner nonetheless.

"Crossroads is the place I've spent the last few years."

"It was your home?" He raised his head, his lips leaving the pulse on her neck. His eyes pierced hers, seeking understanding.

"No." She let the word out with all the vile vehemence of the emotions that she felt. "I was taken from my family home after all of them were slaughtered in a territorial dispute. Every single one, killed. I wasn't there when it happened. When I came home, I found total devastation."

Her bear sensed his reaction, smelled his anger and dismay at the helplessness of her plight. Yet he didn't say a word; instead, he waited for her to finish.

"Except that the marauders weren't gone. They took me captive."

Sara paused and listened for Ivan. She heard his sweet giggle, heard the baritones of the other shifters in the room with him and knew she could continue her recounting safely.

Ivan was in good hands, better than hers, her bear reminded her.

"I was sold to a hospital." She shook her head as the memory of that first day came back to her. She'd shifted into her bear, and fought, but they'd drugged her. They'd shot some kind of drug into her with a dart. She'd fallen and her bear had gone deep inside her. From that day on, they'd kept Sara on some kind of drug that kept her from shifting.

Sara realized she'd drifted into her own memories and stopped talking when Joe began to stroke her hair.

"After the hospital..." he prompted her.

She needed to sum it up and not dwell on it, for her own wellbeing.

"There was no 'after the hospital,' not for a long time. The hospital had a laboratory. I was kept on some sort of drug that paralyzed my body. It kept me from shifting, but I was fully awake."

Awake when they took my virginity. Awake when I

became pregnant with Ivan. She bit back the bitter tears that threatened.

Ivan was the only good thing that had come from that place.

"And Ivan?" Joe wasn't slow putting things together, it seemed.

Sara nodded. "I was drugged. Every day."

Joe clenched his jaw, his muscles working, the tendons in his neck drawing tight, the pulse in his temple throbbing. She didn't have to tell him more. He understood.

"How did you get away?"

"Something happened when I became pregnant with Ivan. The drugs became less potent as each day passed. Or maybe my immunity changed while I was pregnant. All I knew was that my bear was finally able to come out. She'd been locked away for so long." She bit back a sob.

Joe wrapped his arms around her, holding her tight, murmuring sounds of comfort, sounds that reached into her so deeply that her bear was embraced.

"Joe, it was like she was under many, many inches of ice. I could see her, but I couldn't reach her. I couldn't talk to her. For all my life as far back as I can remember, my bear had been a part of me. She was my best friend and my sister. Then they did that to me, and I couldn't bring her out. I couldn't talk to her. Not even in my mind."

Joe squeezed her, keeping her and her bear

ensconced in his muscular arms, his long dark hair making a curtain that cocooned them from the world.

"That's one of the reasons I don't mind being in my bear so much more than my human skin. It's her turn."

Joe nodded, the side of his face pressing against her head. She inhaled his scent, let her bear relish the scent of him, the man of him, and the mate of him.

Her bear breathed a sigh of relief deep inside Sara. Tears formed in Sara's eyes. Tears of joy, though she couldn't figure out why she was happy.

"And Ivan?" Joe's breath was warm on her cheek. "The escape?"

"My bear. She came to help us. I was pregnant with him, heavily so, but by then the drugs couldn't contain her. So when the time was right, she came to our rescue." Sara rubbed her face with the blanket, brushing the tears away with the soft fabric. "She killed—we killed—three men. I must not be found. I'm wanted for murder, I'm sure."

"So you stay in your bear form. And you gave birth to Ivan? Alone?"

"No, not alone. My bear was there. She helped me make it through. And Ivan was born like that. A bear cub. And there was no reason to teach him to shift. There was every reason not to."

"He's about four. You've been on the run since then?"

Sara straightened her posture while still in his arms.

"We've managed." She was proud of how far they'd come.

"But you're being hunted? Why else would you keep going from place to place?"

"We were found once, two years ago. We stay on the move."

"Where is Crossroads?"

"Canada."

"Where in Canada?"

"How would I know exactly? I was incapacitated. I couldn't move. I didn't have access to a map. To anything. I know I went south and east. So I guess it's north and west from here. More north. And I did travel along the coast." She'd blocked so much of this. She didn't want to remember this stuff at all. She wished Joe wouldn't pry. It wasn't like she'd ever planned on returning.

And now for the bad news.

"Joe, I need to go. I'm healed. I need to get on the road. I have to do a lot of training with Ivan, now that he knows how to shift. I have to prepare him for new things, new instances or dangers that might arise."

His hand, formerly resting against the inside of her thigh, curved around her leg now, gripping her. Not tight, but not casually. The hand under her ass tightened as well. The tendons in his muscles became rigid as his body flexed.

"I can't let you do that, Sara." His whispered words elicited fear and joy. Fear that by not being on the move she and Ivan were in grave danger. Fear that Joe would be risking his life. Joy that she mattered to him.

A sadness crept through her. She mattered to a man she couldn't have. She had to go. Immediately. She had to take danger away from him. She had to keep Ivan safe. If Crossroads got their hands on Ivan… She didn't let her mind go there. She couldn't think of that now. She couldn't live with that kind of knowledge.

She might have killed one of the doctors, but there were a panel of them that ran Crossroads. More than half a dozen doctors had come in regularly to monitor their testing and her reaction. They drew blood, tested, poked, prodded, and took slivers of flesh from different areas of her body.

She'd asked them more than once what they were doing.

"Perfecting your species." That was all they ever said.

"Did you hear me?" Joe took his hand out from underneath the blanket and put it on her chin, turning her head to face him. "Did you hear what I said? Did you?"

She put her hand on his, wrapped her hand around it—only his was so much larger, she couldn't cover it. She moved his hand off her face and put it on her knee, lacing her fingers with his.

"You can't keep me here. You can't keep me prisoner. I'll never be a prisoner again." She leveled her gaze on his, let him see her bear, let him hear her words. "Are you saying you'll try to keep me captive?" She knew the answer to that, but she had to let him see how his words could affect her.

"Never." His words were a low hiss. "I'll let you go." He helped her off his lap.

CHAPTER TWELVE

Joe helped Sara up. She was being foolish. Leaving the protection that Bear Canyon Valley shifters could offer her was folly, but he understood her perspective, and she'd been captive, essentially tied down for too long. She couldn't stay.

Sara held the blanket's ends tight, her hand a fist just above her left breast, clutching the material. He studied her face, rememorizing it for the thousandth—no, the millionth time.

He swallowed hard at the dryness in his throat. He watched her take a breath and hold it. Her chest swelled, her nostrils flared. Her eyes dilated and turned a gold color.

She turned his way, facing him, and dropped the blanket. "I can't go without knowing." She exhaled. "Just once in my life."

"Knowing?" He had to hear the words. He needed to hear every word she was going to say.

"I have to know what it's like to have the man I love inside me. I have to know what it feels like to make love. To be made love to. If only once." Tears highlighted the golden amber.

Joe cracked. Just fucking cracked, right down the middle. He had an animal side to him, no less than she did. He couldn't shift, he couldn't adopt an animal's skin or ways, but he was no less connected to the elements than she.

He put his hands on her shoulders and pulled her against him. He slid his hands down her bare arms and lowered his head. He locked his lips with hers and let her see the passion, the hunger, the eternity of him.

His tongue demanded the same of her.

Sara moaned. His breath mingled with hers, his tongue danced around hers, pulling her deeper into an abyss where there was only her... and him... Tongues tangling, sharing breath, she kept her eyes open, focused on his, reaching deep into the windows of his soul.

His groan was captured by her mouth, but still it took her to a place where she wanted to go.

There was too much between them. Too much fabric. His clothing. She and her bear couldn't be passive. They couldn't be submissive and wait. Not now. Now was the time that Sara wanted to claim him.

She unbuttoned his shirt while her mouth stayed locked on his, their tongues rubbing and twisting. She grasped his shirt and tugged. Understanding what she wanted, he moved his arms and she helped him out of the sleeves. The garment fell to the floor unheeded.

She reached for his pants. With an unpracticed and fumbled yet quick twist, she had the button released and the zipper down. She tugged them off his hips. His pants fell to the floor, and he stepped out of them.

Her body quivered with longing for him. A furnace burned in her core. Only he could quench the molten need that filled her.

How had this man reached into her and pulled her soul so close to his in this short time period? Was it short? It felt like she'd known him for an eternity. What resonated with Sara the most was how fiercely her bear was in love with him. Sara had no idea—had never thought this was possible—to feel for him, and to have her bear love him so deeply.

It was wonderfully thrilling. And if she wasn't worried about the danger that Crossroads presented, she could yield to the emotions and take what Joe had to offer.

But she couldn't let her guard down. She had to keep moving. She'd take everything she could right now, and keep it for an eternity.

Joe's hands slid down her shoulders, lowering and cupping her ass, pulling her tight to him. She put her hands on his stomach, his abs tight under her fingers. She ran her fingernails over the flesh of his chest, the fullness of his pecs, up to the wide set of his shoulders.

Joe groaned. He pulled away from the kiss. His hands lowered, cupping her full breasts just beneath the mounds. His thumbs resting on her nipples, and he rubbed circles on the pebbled, dark brown tips.

The moisture deep within her pussy began to make its journey downward. It would only be a matter of seconds before the proof of her lust for him was a mess between her thighs. She smelled his desire, smelled the drop of pre-cum that had already presenting itself on his thickness and been rubbed onto her belly when he'd pulled her close. She lowered her hand to her stomach, found it, ran her thumb over it and put it in her mouth.

"Ah, fuck, Sara," he growled.

"I had to see how you taste. I have to know."

"Christ." He squeezed her breasts with his hands, then pinched her nipples between his fingers and rolled them, then pinched them flat. The pain was perfect, exquisite, and rolled through her body like thunder.

"I want you," Sara admitted. "I've never wanted a man. I've never known this could happen." How could she possibly explain to him that she'd never so much as gotten wet over a man? That life had never even presented that opportunity? She'd never had a sex drive.

And now? It was like she was in heat for him. She wanted him. All of him. Every inch of him. He occupied her mind, her body. She wanted him in her with a ferocity that was scary.

"Touch me."

She lowered her hand. Touched the hard length of him. Felt the hotness of his flesh. She held him tight in her hand, then moved her hand up and down his cock. At the base of it, she wrapped her hand around it and squeezed.

He groaned and pinched her nipple with renewed fervor.

She ran her fingertips up his cock, let her thumb find the slit at the end, slick with his pre-cum. She rubbed it over the head of his cock, making him catch his breath, a low growl coming from deep within his chest.

She lowered herself to her knees. His eyes were focused on hers, then on her lips, his gaze not wavering. She licked her lips and wrapped her hand around him. She felt unsure, but let her emotions guide her. Her body shook, her ache for him rocking her, turning her inside out. She parted her lips, then opened her mouth wide, letting the underside of his cock lay on her tongue. She marveled at the heaviness, the thickness, the rigidity. She closed her lips, feeling the velvety texture of him against the roof of her mouth and her tongue. Pushing her head forward, she let him slide further in, wanting as much as she could take of the smooth length of him.

His eyes narrowed, and a mask of pure lust flashed over his features, making her need for him greater. Her pussy flexed, and her juices ran down her thighs. She flicked her tongue side to side, licking him while he stretched her mouth.

"Ah, Sara. Fuck." Joe's words were an aphrodisiac, the tone so low, the desperation so evident, as if he'd been waiting for this for an eternity. His fingers glided into her hair and he gripped her locks, pulling back, pushing her head forward at the same time.

His groans, the way his head was thrown back, and the tensing and flexing muscles on his stomach were the encouragement she needed that he liked what she was doing. She moved her head back and forth, his length slick with her saliva.

He pulled her up, her body going upward as his spit-slickened cock left a trail on her chest, then her abdomen. He kissed her while she wrapped her hands around his cock, pulling on him, jerking on him, imagining that this would be what her pussy would be doing to him if they were fucking.

He put both hands under her and raised her upwards while turning at the same time. Her back was against the wall, her chest against Joe, her legs wrapped around him and hooked on his hips.

"I can't wait. I fucking need you. Now."

She wanted to tell him she felt the same way. She couldn't tell him that; it would be her undoing. It would put her in a position where she'd have to follow through on her emotions. So instead, she tugged him closer with her legs.

With one swift drive, he plunged into her. She gasped from the way his width stretched her. He pressed his lips to hers, drinking her gasp away. It felt like he was touching every part of her, from her pelvis to her throat. She wrapped her arms around his neck and pulled herself closer, latching onto his lips, driving her tongue into his mouth the way he was diving into her. Her pussy clenched around him, her muscles contracting with pleasure.

Joe stopped. Froze. He grabbed her ass tighter, pulling her onto him until their joining was seamless. Completely still, he breathed her in.

"Don't move," she said. "I want to remember this moment forever."

He frowned as if absorbing her words and picking up the meaning.

"Forever. That's how long you'll be mine." He groaned and began to pump, stroking in and out. She clawed at his shoulders, raked her nails down his biceps, scored his chest as she flailed, unable to control the spasms taking over her body.

"Be still, Sara, or you're going to make me—" Joe pulled away, but Sara's bear and Sara both reacted, holding him, ramming her back onto him, fully, totally, completely impaled.

He reared back and pulled away, just enough to partially come out of her, and turned toward the bed. Sara grasped his shoulders, pulling herself up, and sliding back down on him. The friction between them, the adrenaline, the emotions were too much.

Her mind was muddled. Her breath came out in bursts and pants. She clawed at his shoulders, searching for purchase while her body began to come undone, falling further and further into a chasm that was exploding with tiny pinpoints of light, more intense than the fireworks she'd seen when she was a child.

"No other man will have this. It's mine. You're mine."

His words touched her, grabbed her, and threw her over an orgasmic cliff. She opened her mouth to scream for him, and he swooped down, catching her scream, taking it into his lungs.

While she was still in the middle of contractions and aftershocks, Joe held her tight, carried her to the bed, and flipped her over.

He ran his hand along her spine, his fingertips burning a trail into her flesh. She couldn't concentrate. Her mind was short-circuited from one aftershock after another. She'd never imagined that sex could ever be so intense and freeing.

Joe's hand slipped around her hip, over her waist, cupping her sex, sliding his fingers between her already slick and still spasming folds.

"Fuck, you feel incredible." He grunted the words

out, raw and sexy, as his fingers parted her lips and rubbed fast circles on her clit.

Sara moaned, unable to put the words together to tell him how he was affecting her and how she felt about him.

With a quick thrust, he plowed into her, stretching her again, filling her completely, and pressing against her already heightened G-spot.

She shoved her hips back, taking him in as deep as she could, and rolled her pussy. Joe groaned, pumping his shaft, ratcheting up the level of arousal, pushing her closer and closer to the place she'd never been to with anyone else.

He pulled back, taking away the heat of his body, leaving her wanting more. When he drove into her again, she pushed back, enjoying the give and take of his thrusts. She moaned low with every thrust, while he slapped a hand on her hip.

His powerful plunges increased in tempo. All she could hear was the sound of her breathing, her low moans, and the slapping of his skin against hers. He angled his hips and fucked her with sweeping strokes.

"Christ." He held still for a moment.

"Don't stop." The words were ripped from her very core.

"If I don't, I'm liable to—"

She didn't care. All she knew was that she wanted

him fiercely. She began to push her body back and forth, impaling herself over and over.

With that, Joe's self-control seemed to vanish. It felt like he grew more engorged, filling her while a part of her snapped. She felt his orgasm, hot and fluid, deep within her. She bit her lip to contain the screech of her own orgasm while her pussy milked the cum from his shaft.

He collapsed on her. His teeth sank into her, just where her shoulders met her neck.

She lost sensation in her legs and collapsed. He lay on her, his body heaving from the exertion and the climax.

A rumbling sound caught her attention.

It wasn't her bear.

It was his stomach. It occurred to her that she hadn't eaten either.

"I want you to meet everyone, anyway," Joe said.

CHAPTER THIRTEEN

Sara put on the dress Joe handed her. Now, more than ever, she was happy that he'd bought them some clothing. She could never pay him back, though, and she felt bad about that. Maybe one day she'd be able to, when she didn't have to stay hidden. When she wasn't worried about Ivan.

Joe was already dressed and sitting in the chair, waiting for her to finish dressing. His stomach's protests and her own stomach cramps were enough to convince her that she needed to get some sustenance.

She was ready to see Ivan. To watch him in his human form.

Joe opened the door and escorted her down a hallway. They followed the scent of the food. Delicious-smelling food.

Sara could hear the laughter coming from the kitchen. One of those voices was her own baby's, in his human form. He giggled, a high-pitched sound of merriment. First she saw Ivan, playing with three shifters.

She recognized one. He was the one who'd been with the woman in the cave a few weeks ago. The woman who'd held Ivan against her body and given Sara a challenging look, as if she would protect Ivan from a strange bear.

She was a brave human, taking on a bear, especially when she didn't know I was a shifter. A good—or bad —shifter.

Next to him was the brave woman herself.

Yes, that was her, the one who'd held Ivan in the tunnel. And that was definitely the man who'd been with her.

The shifter that Sara had wounded. Sara paused for a moment, studying the couple, noting the bond they clearly had. Of course they had a bond; the male had jumped to her defense that day in the forest.

What they didn't know was that Sara had seen them making love. She fought to keep a blush from rising to her cheeks and pushed her thoughts away from the vision that was still fresh in her mind, a vision that made her think about what she and Joe had just done. She felt the heat intensify in her cheeks as embarrassment flourished in her mind. She needed to stop that thought process right now. She shook it off and looked at her son.

Ivan was drinking in the attention, his cheeks flushed a happy pink color, his smile wide. Then he saw her.

"Mama." He ran toward her and wrapped his arms around her legs. "I have new friends. And I know how to shift back and forth from my bear to this." He beamed up at her, indicating his body with a gesture.

"I see that. I'm proud of you." She ruffled his hair, leaned down and gave him a hug, kissing his cheek. She was overwhelmed by Ivan's appearance in his human skin. It would take some getting used to.

She glanced at the shifter she'd attacked that day in the forest. "I know you."

"Teague." He pointed to his chest. "Teague Navarro."

"I'm sorry." She made a sad grimace. "I didn't mean to hurt you. I didn't know... wasn't sure..."

"You did what was natural. Completely understood." Teague smiled, then pointed to the woman who'd held Ivan that day. "This is Kelsey."

The curvy, beautiful woman next to him smiled. "Ivan's a charmer." She held out her hand.

Sara rose and took the hand for a shake. "Don't I know it."

Kelsey held her hand, not letting go. "That day. I'm sorry. I didn't know. I had no clue, and my mind went toward helping the baby bear."

Sara nodded, sensing there was more but not sure what. "I'd have probably done the same thing if I were in your shoes."

A wave of sadness passed over Kelsey's face. Sara didn't want to pry. She diverted quickly.

"I'm Kane. This is Astra," the other shifter in the room said, and indicated a woman with eyes so green, so clear it was as if they were lit from behind.

"Doc's my father, well... stepfather," the green-eyed woman said, turning to the third shifter in the room, putting her arm around him. Clearly they were a close-knit group.

"Thank you." Sara turned to the doctor shifter. "You saved my life."

"Glad I was around."

She addressed the group of them. "Thank you for looking after Ivan while I was recuperating."

"Oh, he's a pleasure. We enjoy having a little shifter around. Now we have two."

"Two?" Sara asked.

"My brother's mate has a son. His name is Dominic. I think he and Ivan would get along great."

That will never happen. I need to get out of here as quickly as possible. Especially now that I know there's a little shifter who would be in danger from Crossroads as well.

"I'm sure they would," Sara said, hating herself for lying to these people, especially after their kindness.

Sara was saved by her stomach. It rumbled so loud that even the humans heard it. Astra and Kelsey burst into laughter.

"Let's eat." Kelsey indicated a table full of food. "Mae

brought some over, but she couldn't stay. After closing the shop, she was taking some soup to Tanner and Marti."

"What would we ever do without Mae?" Kane laughed.

"Indeed." Doc's voice was low.

Sara studied the handsome doctor shifter, then turned her glance to the other two shifters. She hadn't been around this many shifters... any shifters, really, since... She pushed the memories away and took the plate that Kelsey handed her.

Joe sat next to her. She had a heightened sense of his body next to hers. It was as if they were connected by an invisible field of energy. Her own body pulsed with awareness of his, of what they'd done, of the feelings he brought out in her.

Hell, she wished it was as simple as the words "brought out." Joe didn't just bring feelings out. He completely and totally overwhelmed her senses. Everything was amplified with him next to her.

A shiver ran through her. She should run away as fast as she could. This was too much, too real, too... She couldn't even come up with the words. *Yes, I've got to get out of here. Like, quickly.* She glanced out the cabin's window. It was still light outside. She'd leave as soon as it was dark, when everyone was gone. She'd sneak away like a thief in the night.

I suck. I really suck. Can't believe I'd do that to him.

Her bear growled in agreement.

I don't want to hear your thoughts on it. You know they're all better off with me gone.

Especially Joe.

CHAPTER FOURTEEN

Sara breathed easily for the first time in a long time. And it wasn't lost on her that she'd not had this kind of peace since she was a child.

The easy camaraderie of the shifters and their mates was comforting. Ivan was in his element with the group, enjoying the attention, showing his mother how he'd learned to shift back and forth, quickly, easily, and seamlessly. Sara bit back the tears as she watched her little one showing off his newly learned skill.

"Look, Mama." He growled and shifted again into a little bear, stood on his hind legs and let out a roar.

"That's wonderful."

I hate that I have to take you away from all this and back to a miserable life on the road with just your mother for company.

Joe's dark gaze bored into her. She wondered if he could read her mind.

Of course not, don't be silly, she chastised herself.

But yet, there was something about the way he watched her, as if he knew something. As if he were privy to her darkest secrets.

"So, where are you from?" Kelsey asked.

Sara froze. *Here we go.* The questions she didn't want to answer.

"She's from Canada," Joe answered.

"What shifter family?" Kane put his fork in his mouth, but the tone that he'd used raised a question within Sara.

"I don't have a family." Sara hoped her tone would dissuade more conversation on the topic.

But it didn't. They all stared at her, waiting.

Fine, but I'm not going into detail and I'm not telling them about Crossroads. "They were killed."

"That's something many of us have experience with," Astra said, her eyes glowing. "You'll be safe here." She said it with such assurance that Sara had to wonder why she was so sure.

"She's right," Doc agreed. "There are several of us, and among us we have a network of friends that extends across several continents."

She wasn't going to risk their lives to find out if they really could keep her safe. She wasn't going to do that to them. And she wasn't doing that to Joe. They simply didn't understand. And she couldn't explain Crossroads to them.

"This is great." She pointed to the pot roast with her fork. "Tell Mae thank you." She wondered who Mae was.

"You'll get a chance to tell her yourself." Doc glanced at his phone. "She said she'd stop by after she closed up shop and delivered the soup."

"You're staying for a while, right?" Astra got straight to the point.

"I'm not sure."

"Yes, Mama, let's stay." Ivan shoved a piece of garlic toast in his mouth. "I like it here and I want to meet Dominic. He has a cold right now, but he'll be better tomorrow, maybe."

Great. Just damned great.

Sara looked down so she wouldn't be giving anyone a dirty look. This was not working out at all. Now Ivan was on their side.

Their side? She immediately felt horrible for thinking this way. They'd done nothing but help her and Ivan. Her bear grumbled agreement with that thought.

Yeah, when you've been on your own as long as I have, you get this way.

Her bear snarled.

I know you were there. You don't know what I mean. I was helpless. Powerless. Completely under someone else's control.

Her bear released a roar that made Sara want to hold her hands over her ears.

I know. I'm sorry. I should have thought about it from your perspective. You were just as powerless. And you couldn't help me. I'm sorry.

She was sorry. She realized it couldn't have been easy for her bear to sit back and watch her being manipulated, tortured, pried, prodded, and even raped.

"Sara?" It was Joe.

Everyone was staring at her, concern on their faces. She realized they'd been talking to her. Had they asked her a question?

"Sorry. Lost in thought." She glanced at Joe.

The way he was looking at her made her nervous. She couldn't get over the feeling that he knew what was in her mind. In her heart.

"I was saying you could stay with us," Kelsey repeated. "I run the Bed & Breakfast for Mae. We always have rooms reserved for special visitors." She smiled at Ivan. "You two are very special visitors."

"How far along are you?" Sara asked. She'd scented Kelsey's baby, and she could hear the baby's heart beating strong inside its mother.

Kelsey gasped.

Teague burst into laughter.

Astra squealed.

Kane and Doc exchanged knowing looks and smiles.

"It was a secret." Kelsey's voice was a high-pitched, excited one.

"Like I didn't know." Teague took her hand.

"I don't think I like this. I can't even surprise you with the good news," she huffed.

"Maybe you should have told me." Kelsey gave Teague a mock frown.

Sara felt bad. "I'm sorry. I didn't realize it wasn't public already."

"It's okay." Kelsey reached across and put her hand on Sara's arm. "We really don't have many secrets from each other. It's better that way." She drew a deep breath in. "I guess a part of me was keeping it quiet because of the last time." She looked at Teague. "I lost our baby more than two years ago. It was a rough time. When I saw Ivan that day, I was just coming to grip with certain emotions."

Now Sara understood the sadness that had crossed over her face. "I'm sorry."

Teague put his arm around Kelsey. "We've come to terms with it. We know there was probably a reason that it happened and we don't question it anymore." He kissed Kelsey on the forehead and put his hand on her tummy. "Everything's better now."

Kelsey nodded.

Tears welled up in Sara's eyes. She pushed them back. She was happy for what they had, and sad she didn't have that, and never would. She wondered if she and Joe could ever have had that.

Feeling eyes on her, Sara looked up.

Joe.

His eyes were almost black, his gaze intense. He was looking toward the window. "I'll be back in a bit. Something I need to take care of."

Kane and Teague gave him a look as he pushed his chair back from the table. Sara wondered what that look was about.

He was just leaving? Just like that? Leaving her alone? It wasn't that she didn't trust all of them, for they gave the vibes off that she could trust them with her life... but still... it was Joe's home and she was his guest.

He ruffled Ivan's hair and said, "See you soon, little man." He grabbed a set of keys from the table next to the door and headed out.

"Bye, Joe," Ivan called out. "See you soon."

Odd. What the hell? Just like that, he was gone? "He's coming back soon, like he said, right?" she asked the others.

"Probably. Not sure what he's going to do." Doc frowned, giving a sidelong glance to Kane and Teague.

Something about this worried her. But what could she do? She could be ungracious and leave with Ivan right now, and not get to say goodbye to Joe, or she could have a few moments with him this evening and leave in the middle of the night.

Like a criminal, her bear reminded her.

Sara ignored it. She wasn't up to arguing with her bear. Not now. She couldn't deal with her bear, her emotions about leaving, and her emotions for Joe all at the same time. She had to pick her battles.

She rose from her seat and went to the window to see if she could get a glimpse of Joe. "I wonder what's so important he had to go." She had a feeling the shifters knew something.

She saw movement and turned her head in that direction. The first thing she noticed was Joe's truck. Then she saw a form.

It was Joe, reaching into his truck. She bit back a gasp when she saw he'd pulled out a box with a handle. She knew what kind of box that was. That it housed a rifle. What would he be doing with a rifle?

She kept watching. He leaned in again and pulled out...

A pair of tomahawks? Really? Did those things even exist except in tourist areas and kids' toys? *Shows how much I know. I guess I've never really been around any Native American people. Not the kind who would carry or have any of those.*

She turned back to the shifters at the table. She knew better than to think that Joe was hunting. Not now. Not while everyone was here. "Why would Joe have a rifle?"

"Joe used to be a sniper." Doc's words were matter-of-fact.

"I thought he was in the rodeo," Kelsey said. "That's what Marti told me."

"He was that too, but he was a sniper before that. One of the best, according to Grant. Not that Joe will talk about it."

So why is he taking a rifle out? Sara didn't like where this was making her mind go.

"I think I'll take a walk." She had to find out what Joe was up to. For some reason it plagued her greatly. She looked at Kelsey. "Can I leave Ivan with you?"

"Of course. Always." Kelsey got up from the table and picked up a book. "Let's read, Ivan."

"Kelsey." Sara choked on the lump that had decided to set up residence in her throat.

"Yes?" Ivan in her lap, Kelsey looked up from the book they were reading.

"Nothing." Sara turned away, then abruptly turned back. "I don't have family." She swallowed hard, willing the lump away, but it only grew bigger and bigger. "I don't have anyone. If anything ever happened..."

"Hey, now," Kane said.

Astra put her arm around her. "Nothing's going to happen. I promise you."

That's a promise you can't keep. You have no idea what I'm up against.

She had to get the thought out. "Seriously. If anything should. Ivan... I'd like..."

Fuck. Fuck!

She couldn't get the words out. She tried to clear her throat but it was too dry and there was nothing to clear it with.

"I will," Kelsey said.

That was all Kelsey said, but it was all that Sara needed. "Thank you." She knelt and kissed Ivan on his head. His hair was soft against her lips. She fought back the urge to squeeze him with all her might, to shift and take him away from the world.

God damn the Crossroads people.

She had to go see what Joe was up to. And make sure he wasn't wandering a forest alone, where he could be hurt.

CHAPTER FIFTEEN

In camouflage, his face completely marked up to hide his flesh, barely visible even to the fauna in the forest, Joe surveyed the men with the scope. He was high up in a tree, one of the many spots in the forest that he'd identified over the years, growing up here, making his way around with his grandfather.

He pulled the scope into a tighter focus. Four men. All the men who had been there. All dead. None remained alive to interrogate or to follow. Joe had killed them from about as far away as he used to shoot when he was in the military.

Haven't lost the touch.

Killing wasn't something he was proud of, but it was something he was good at. He knew they'd been up to no good. He'd watched them follow Sara's tracks. Shooting them wasn't a tough decision to make. He'd shoot damn near anyone to protect Sara and Ivan.

Finding them had been easy. He raised his eyes skyward, thankful for the gifts he'd received from his grandfather. The ability to read the forest and be in touch with its creatures was something he'd never taken for granted. It was also something he'd never appreciated as much as he did now.

Joe had studied the men. The way they'd carried themselves and the way their clothes were creased and tucked gave away a military training.

All of them had been armed with pistols. Clearly not your average hunters. They were hunters of men. Or in this case, a woman and a child.

Silly, he thought, for them not to have something more powerful. In her bear form, those pistols wouldn't even be able to slow Sara down, not in the least.

Unless the pistols didn't have rounds in them. Unless they had whatever it was that had made her unable to shift or move. He sneered, a look of disgust curling his lip and marking his handsome face.

Anyone who would do that to a woman was beneath contempt. Yes, he'd find them. All these men who came to his territory and tried to hurt the ones he loved.

A security team, surely sent from Crossroads.

He'd find out more about Crossroads and its location and those in charge of it later. Right now he'd take care of the issues at hand: the men in his territory.

There were more of these men. He hadn't found a vehicle, not yet, but he would. He'd find the others and he'd take care of them. Then he'd return to his cabin and make Sara his. He'd take good care of her and Ivan, give them the lives they deserved.

He shouldered his rifle and climbed down the tree he'd been in, making his way down with the ease of one practiced in maneuvering in trees and forests.

Making his way through the densely treed forest with stealth, Joe kept his awareness heightened. He wasn't sure if the others were hiding or tracking. He let nature show him the signs of their path in the form of broken twigs, displaced leaves and an occasional missed boot print. Police issue, it looked like.

Joe's extra senses picked up a sound. Controlling his pulse, he leaned against a bush and made himself one with the forest while he waited for the source of the sound.

Half a dozen men marched by, more interested in their conversation while the head man tracked Sara. They were headed for his cabin. Not good.

"I'd like to find her before dark," one of the men said.

"We will. These tracks aren't old," another said.

That completely summed it up for Joe. They were after Sara.

Would he take all of them on with a rifle? That wouldn't do. His rifle was better from a distance. He only had one pair of tomahawks, and there were half a dozen men here.

These odds suck.

He wasn't stupid. He'd wait. Biding his time had always been one of his strengths. He let the men get ahead of him. They wouldn't be a problem to keep up with. He could intercept them and take them out one at a time before they arrived at his cabin.

"I don't like this," Sara muttered. She wasn't crazy about the idea of Joe wandering about in a forest that might have Crossroads goons in it.

She heard a noise, then felt heartbeats, and froze. Sara held her breath. She was prepared to kill and even be killed if it would put an end to the hunt. If it would keep her son safe. If it would keep Joe alive.

She shifted into her bear and stood in between two large pine trees. The wind teased the pine needles near her ear, but she didn't let it interfere with her concentration. Low, rustling sounds came from the left: soft steps in the soil and an occasional leaf being crushed. Her bear's intensity was riveted to whatever was approaching.

Sara poised, mighty bear arms raised, claws ready to deal lethal blows.

"It's us." Kane's voice.

She shifted into her human form quickly. "What are you doing here?"

Kane, Teague, and Doc appeared from between the trees.

"You're not serious." Teague frowned. "You're one of us."

A burning in her eyes made her curse the response she had to his words. Damn Teague for saying the one thing that would make her emotional. She bit the tears back and the burn migrated to the bridge of her nose.

"Plus, Ivan needs his mama." Teague smiled. She could see what Kelsey saw in this man, though no man had the same effect on her that Joe did.

Joe. Damn that hardheaded man. "We need to find Joe."

"What are you worried about, Sara?" Doc frowned at her. "Who could be a threat to Joe out here? This is our forest. Our land, our territory. No shifter in his right mind would challenge that."

"It's not a shifter that worries me."

"Then...?"

"Can we get to Joe first? I'd rather save the explaining for later."

"Sure, but—"

The sound of a shot interrupted Kane.

Then another. And another.

Sara flinched with each shot.

Doc's face grew serious.

"Shit," Teague hissed.

"Fuck," Kane added.

"Shift," Doc said. "Now."

All four of them shifted immediately, and began at a loping pace in the direction of the shots.

Sara found that she couldn't breathe. She was too worried about Joe. She backed up and surrendered her body to her bear, if only for a moment or two while she tried to grab control of herself.

They found the first four bodies. Dead for a few minutes at least. Sara looked at them closely and pawed at one, turning him over so she could see his face. She knew that face from Crossroads.

These men had been dead a lot longer than the brief time since the shots rang out.

There were more.

Was Joe okay? How many more were there?

Doc growled for them to keep on the move. The four of them started to move quickly through the forest. Doc took lead, Kane was next, then Sara, while Teague brought up the rear.

A few moments later, they found another body. And another. Pistols were in their belts, blood still pouring out of their bodies.

They all shifted back to their human skin with the slightest creaking and crunching sounds.

As soon as he'd shifted, Kane put a hand on her shoulder. "You don't know how to sync?" he asked.

"What?" Sara was confused.

"We were trying to sync with you and couldn't. Have you never done that?"

"No. I don't know if I can. No one ever taught me how, though."

She'd have to find out more about that one day. *Wait. What the hell am I thinking? There won't be that one day. Ever. I need to get away from here.*

She heard a branch crack. Evidently they all did at the same time, for they all turned toward the area it came from.

A camouflaged, face-painted Joe came down from the tree, landing softly near them. "Guess it's easier than I thought to hide from shifters." He smiled, but Sara could tell his smile was strained.

"Had to kill them. Or they'd go back to Crossroads."

"I'm not mourning." Sara drank in his appearance. She had to contain her thoughts for fear the other three shifters would know what she felt for Joe.

"There are four more," Joe added.

That had the opposite effect of an aphrodisiac on her. Sara's blood ran cold.

"We'll get them." Kane began to shift.

CHAPTER SIXTEEN

"Hey. No one invited you three—four—to my party." Joe hitched the rifle over his shoulder.

He couldn't take his eyes off Sara. Her dark hair was wild, like it had been when he first met her, first talked to her, that day, in her gloriously naked skin. Her face was flushed from running, she was panting, and he couldn't help but remember the sex.

Damn if that didn't work.

His cock twitched. Christ. Bad time to get a hard-on. This woman had some crazy kind of hold on him. He shook his head to clear it.

"Your party?" Her dark rose lips curled into a smile, but beneath the smile was a measure of melancholy. She was leaving him.

He wasn't about to let that happen. Clearly she had no idea who she was dealing with.

"The last four are mine."

"There are five of us," Kane added. "Sucks to be them."

Teague smacked him in the shoulder.

Sara's smile vanished. "I think I deserve the pleasure, after everything I've been through."

Knowing her story, Joe couldn't argue with that, but what if she were hurt?

"I don't want you hurt."

"It's my battle. I think I should be able to claim the pleasure of taking them out."

"I'll be right behind you," Joe told her.

She nodded.

"We will too." Doc shifted.

Kane and Teague shifted too.

Sara shifted into her bear and took off searching for the scent of the men. She could smell their fear. She could smell each one individually, and her bear recognized their scent. Their block must have worn off, because the first ones Joe had killed had had no scent.

Their scent was getting stronger. She was getting closer. Joe was behind her, moving almost completely silently through the undergrowth.

Behind him Kane, Teague, and Doc were taking no measures to hide their approach.

There. She saw one. He was the last one in the line. Then the others came into view. They were heading toward the cabin.

They were heading toward her son, her innocent little boy, and her two unprotected new friends.

She roared her anger and took off for the men, her vision focused on killing them. Her rage made everything appear in shades of red.

All four men turned on her, drawing pistols. Her bear laughed inside at the threat that pistols would pose.

They fired at her. Then she realized those weren't bullets.

At the same moment, four darts sank into her flesh, stinging.

She snarled and pulled at them with her claws, dislodging them. But it was too late. Her vision started to blur, then close in, slowly, like a black kaleidoscope.

Joe resisted the urge to run to Sara. First he had to eliminate the danger. He took the two tomahawks from his belt. Like his grandfather had taught him, long ago, he took aim and released the first one. It landed soundly in the skull of the nearest thug and felled him immediately. He released the second one with equally deadly intensity and knocked the second one off his feet, at the same time killing him.

Behind him, Kane, Teague, and Doc roared and ran forward.

Roars and growls filled the air as the three shifters

rushed the two remaining men while they were reloading their drug-carrying pistols.

Joe pulled his rifle and took aim at the man who was too close to need a scope for anyway. With an ear-deafening shot that was louder than the bears' roars, the man fell, his shirt quickly blossoming with red.

The three shifters were on the last man before Joe could turn on him. They swung, digging claws into the thug, ripping his arm off. His scream was cut short as Kane bit down on his neck, severing his spine and arteries.

The man collapsed, dead, shredded, bloody.

CHAPTER SEVENTEEN

Sara's world was groggy. She wanted to rub her eyes but couldn't. She opened them. She couldn't shake her head. Was she back at Crossroads? Why couldn't she move? What about Ivan?

"Where..." She couldn't even get the words out fully to ask where she was.

Ivan. Where was he? What had happened to Ivan? She couldn't breathe. She fought to get air into her lungs.

Her bear roared in her head. Sara couldn't hear anything else because of her bear. She tried to ignore her, and finally her bear stopped.

"Sara."

Joe's voice? She couldn't turn her head to see.

"Joe." Her voice sounded like a frog's croak.

"Sara. You're with us. You're fine. Ivan's fine. He's sleeping next to you. They shot you with drugs. They're going to wear off. Doc said you'll be fine within a few hours. All of the Crossroads team is dead."

Sara's vision became blurry. She knew it was tears. She felt Joe wiping them away from her cheeks. He leaned in, close, and his mouth alit on hers in the most tender, lightest of touches.

"You're both safe." He brushed her hair off her face.

Until the next Crossroads team decides to arrive. Now, more than ever, she knew she had to get out of the area. She couldn't endanger the shifters here. They'd be captured and taken to Crossroads.

She couldn't keep her eyes open. She allowed them to close. She'd think of things later. Right now her head was too fuzzy.

SARA SAT UP. SHE RECOGNIZED JOE'S HOME. THE SAME room they'd... She shouldn't think of that. Joe was sitting across from her in the chair. This was like déjà vu. "How long was I out?"

"Few hours." He looked haggard.

She felt guilty for his strained and pale expression. "You look like hell."

"Been through it before." His face was stoic, not giving away any emotions. "Still going?"

He wasn't wasting any time jumping to the subject on his mind, was he? "I have to."

His jaw worked, the muscles clenching, the tendons stretching clear to his temples. "You can't protect Ivan alone."

"I can't put you all in danger, and I don't want anyone to have to fight my battles."

"What's yours is mine."

"Nice in theory. I'm leaving in the morning."

"So all I have is tonight." Joe's eyes were hooded, his emotions hidden.

She nodded and looked away, at the picture of him and his grandfather. At the intricate carving on the bedposts, at the knickknacks on the dresser. She looked at anything but him. Looking at him would destroy her resolve.

She threw her legs over the side of the bed and put her feet on the floor. Once she was certain she was able to stand on her feet without losing her balance, she made a slow, deliberate pace toward the bedroom door. "I need to see Ivan."

"He's in the front room, on the sofa. Kelsey's watching him."

Sara made her way to the living room, managing to gain lucidity with every step. Ivan was stretched out on the couch, a blanket over his legs. Kelsey was sitting next to his head, her fingers in his hair, her own head flung back as she catnapped while he slept.

She opened her eyes when the board Sara stepped on creaked.

"Sara. You're awake." Kelsey's smile was sleepy. "He'll be happy to see you."

"We've never been apart as much as we have the last few..." Had it been days or hours? It was a blur for Sara. "It's been difficult."

"I can only imagine." Kelsey rose. "Take my spot."

Sara impulsively hugged her before she sat down. "Thank you for caring for my baby. You have no idea how much it means to me to know he was safe with you."

"We love him. He's such a darling."

Sara held him and closed her eyes. She'd need the rest. She had a long journey to face.

CHAPTER EIGHTEEN

Sara put her fingers over Ivan's lips. They were still on the couch, where she'd fallen asleep. "Shhh. Don't say a word."

She picked him up and carried him to the front door. She opened it slowly, careful not to make any sounds, then slipped out and pulled it just until it touched the jamb, without letting the latch click.

She released a slow sigh of relief that she'd made it outside without detection. Then came the longer sigh. The sigh of heartbreak. She'd never see Joe again.

It's for the best.

Her bear grumbled, disagreeing.

In the night's cool air, she made her way through the trees, using the slight moonlight to guide them, though she didn't really need it.

When she'd judged they were far enough away, she put Ivan down on the ground.

"We need to be bears again."

"Always? Like before?" His voice was sad.

"I'm afraid so."

THEY'D TRAVELED FOR WHAT FELT LIKE FOREVER. IVAN looked tired, his little bear eyes drooping, his legs shuffling, struggling to make the journey.

She'd shift and carry him. She stopped and sat on her haunches. Ivan stopped and looked at her, a question in his eyes.

She shifted into her human form. He followed suit.

"I know you're tired." She hugged him. "I'm sorry."

"Why do I have to be in my bear?"

"It's safer for us that way. No one questions seeing a mama bear and her baby in the woods. But they'd question seeing humans. You understand?"

"I do. But why are we leaving Joe? And Uncle Kane and Uncle Teague? They said I'd get to see Dominic this afternoon, Mama. Did they lie to me?"

She was crushed. She sat on a log and heaved a breath, her shoulders slumped. She pulled her little son, who was way too perceptive for his age, into her lap.

"Oh, no. They would never lie to you. Never." She hissed the words with vehemence.

"Is Mama mad at me?" Ivan wrapped little arms around her, pressed his lips to her cheek. "Mama? Why are you crying?"

"I'm sad." Christ. She couldn't keep yielding to her emotions like this. She'd never be able to take care of her son if she was an emotional mess, for Pete's sake.

"I'm sad too." He sniffled.

"Why are you sad?"

"I don't want to leave my new family."

A sensation gripped her heart, pushing her into an abyss of wretchedness. She held on to him fiercely.

"Mama. Too tight."

"I'm sorry. We should get back into our bears and get on the road."

"Why are we moving again?"

To think she'd been thrilled when he'd first shifted into his human form. Now she couldn't deal with the questions that came from him.

"It's safer for our friends. Our family that we're leaving behind."

"Joe, Uncle Kane and Uncle Teague?"

"Yes, and Doc, and Astra, and Kelsey..."

"And Dominic?" His voice was choked up. He clearly had been looking forward to meeting another little shifter like himself.

I'm denying my child happiness.

Her bear grumbled.

But I'm assuring his life. And I'm protecting our friends. And Joe.

Her bear snarled.

I know. If they can knock me out like that again, they can take Ivan from me.

She screamed inside her head, furious with her bear for pointing out the flaw in her plan. Furious with herself for coming up with such a flawed plan. But what else could she do?

She heard a sound. Faint. But not far away. *Damn.*

She wished she had learned how to sync so she could shift and talk to Ivan silently. She put her hand over his mouth and a finger over hers, ordering him to silence with her gestures. She pushed him low, parallel and against the log.

Rising quickly, she lunged for a tree, ready to shift into her bear.

She found herself facing a tomahawk, inches from the point right between her eyes.

She gasped.

"It's me, Sara. Chill."

"Joe." She whispered his name, relieved. Then she shoved him. "You could have killed me with that thing."

"You shouldn't have left."

"What the hell are you doing out here?" She kept her voice low. In her peripheral vision she noticed Ivan had risen and was watching them.

"I can't make you stay." Joe took her hand in his. "But

I'll be damned if I'm going to let you and Ivan leave my life."

Ivan came running toward them and wrapped his arms around Joe's leg. "I missed you."

Traitor.

Then again, Sara's heart and Sara's bear were being just as traitorous as Ivan, for they had leapt with joy when Joe appeared.

She frowned at Joe, crossing her arms over her chest. "So this is it? You're just going to follow me? That's your plan?"

"Forever. Wherever."

"We need to talk."

"No. you need to come home with me, where the Bear Canyon Valley shifters and I can make sure you're safe." His face was impassive in the dark, but his pulse sounded a strong primal beat and was already synchronized to hers.

She looked at him. His eyes were indiscernible, blending with the night's dimness.

"No strings," he added.

"I have strings." She pulled him closer, taking his other hand in hers. "If you think I'm going to be a submissive, little Miss Betty Crocker…"

He laughed, his teeth white in the dark, his face the same sexy face she'd fallen for. The same face she loved watching in the heat of passion.

"Not a damned chance." His lips touched hers with

the gentleness of a summer breeze, then he pulled away. "I think you're going to be a handful, and I can't wait to try containing that handful. It'll be more fun than herding cats or balancing Jell-O on a butter knife."

Ivan tugged on her dress and Joe's pant leg at the same time.

"Does this mean we're going home?"

"It does," she said, looking directly in Joe's eyes.

"There's one more matter," Joe added.

She nodded. There sure was.

CHAPTER NINETEEN

Several days later...

Sara woke in the crook of Joe's arm, cradled, the way they always slept, her back to him. The silence of the night air greeted her. It was still except for the sound of his pulse and hers. Ivan was spending the night at Marti and Tanner's with his newly discovered cousin, as he called Dominic.

Joe's defined abs lay against her lower back, his hard chest on her spine. His treasure trail, that sprinkling of hair that led from his navel to his cock, tickled her back. Joe didn't wear anything to bed.

His sinewy, muscled leg was thrown over her, as always. He made sure he was protecting her, even when he was asleep.

A hardness pressed against her ass cheek, insistent

and in need, even while her man slept. She felt the pulse of his cock, even through her panties, as it pressed against her ass. She moved slightly, allowing his hardness to settle between her ass cheeks.

Joe's breath was warm on her neck. She held her breath, half from anticipation, and half from desire. She should go back to sleep. She shouldn't disturb him.

Tell that to the wetness in my panties. She'd felt the moisture seeping out of her, a telltale sign of her desire. And here he was, right behind her, with the one thing that could completely cure her desire. The muscles in her channel began to flex and release on their own, responding to the ache.

Sara budged again, just a bit, for it was hard to lie still with this level of desire rushing through her body with the speed of a river she'd gone white water rafting on.

As if responding to her restlessness, though still asleep, Joe moved his arm from her waist to her breast, cupping it, his thumb resting on her nipple, creating a current of electricity that traveled clear to her clit and left her buzzing. Her head felt like it was filled with cotton, like it couldn't concentrate on anything but the pureness of the longing she had for him.

Her dark, rosy peak instantly responded, hardening under his thumb. She couldn't control the slight movement of her hips as she pressed herself against his cock. She moved, raising her hips, dislodging her panties, working them down her legs until they were off.

Tilting one hip, she raised her thigh and allowed Joe's cock to drop between her thighs, resting on her. When she lowered her thigh, his hot hardness was captured between her legs, nestled in the crux of the moisture.

Sara dropped one hand between her legs, touching the velvety smoothness of his mushroom head. The tip of it was slick with his nectar. She rubbed her thumb along the slit, enjoying the pungent, earthy scent of him. She explored his cock's head, feeling the slick, velvety texture.

She pushed her lips apart with her fingers, allowing his cock to part her lips and rest there, like a banana in its peel. As she drew her fingers back, she brushed the top of her clit, still hidden in its hood.

A small gasp escaped her at the sensual feeling. Sara let her finger rest on her clit, moving in slow, hard circles as she pressed against her cleft, every so often letting her fingers slide down to caress his engorged head.

On the third pass over his cock, she felt his breathing pattern change. His fingers, earlier resting on her breasts, now took firm hold of her nipple, pinching and rolling it while his hips moved slowly, his cock going back and forth, fucking the inside of her thighs, using her moisture to ease his efforts.

The throbbing between her legs became unbearable. Her breathing hastened, and small pants escaped from her lips. She pushed her hips against him.

Joe pushed her thigh up, and rose behind her on his knees, then he lowered himself while she lay on her side. His cock slid in, guided by his hand around his hard shaft, eased by the amount of moisture she'd created. He sank deep into her, grunting as he stretched her out.

Her tightness had just wrapped around his thickness when he pulled out and pushed back in, holding on to the leg she'd raised, practically hugging her thigh.

"You're too damned fuckable," Joe groaned between thrusts.

He slid a finger along her moist folds, then slipped it into her, joining his cock.

She whimpered at the new intrusion, then moaned with pleasure as he moved his cock in unison with the finger he'd hooked in her and was pressing against her g-spot.

"I can't get enough of fucking you. I want to fuck every bit of you." He rubbed her lips with his thumb, hooking it and gathering her juices.

He put his thumb on her lips, rubbing her juices in, then pressed, parting the seam of her lips.

"Taste the sweetness of your pussy."

She closed her mouth, savoring her own rich, earthy taste.

Joe groaned as she sucked on his thumb the way she'd suck on his cock, twirling her tongue around it, licking it from side to side.

He took his thumb out and put it back on her pussy,

rubbing her clit, grabbing more moisture while he pumped her over and over.

Sara flinched and did a small jump when she felt his thumb making tiny circles near her ass, but the intensity of his driving deep into her channel, constantly pushing her toward an orgasm, made anything else he did irrelevant for a moment.

"One day, I'm going to brand this part of you too." His voice was hoarse.

Sara pulled her body away, pushing him out of her, and with her hands on his chest, she pushed him down and climbed onto him, straddling his hips, his cock resting between her folds.

She took his shaft in her hands and guided him in, her eyes closing so she could enjoy the sensation of being filled. Sara flexed her muscles, clenching herself around him, making a tight sheath.

She thrust against him over and over again while he held her hips and thrust his pelvis upward, driving himself deeper and deeper.

"Fuck. You know what this is doing to me," Joe groaned.

"The same thing it's doing to me," Sara panted.

Her muscles tightened around him while he became more engorged and swollen, his body tensing. Sara felt her orgasm building, taking control of her. She started to scream. Joe covered her mouth with his, taking her scream in.

He stiffened and groaned, and Sara felt a hot stream pulsing in her as he began to come undone.

Burying her face in his neck, she sank her canines in deep, taking him as hers, bonding with him.

He groaned his pleasure when she began to lick the wound, her mouth providing a heightened sexual sensation, taking the pain away, healing his wound.

"That's to make sure you're always by my side," she whispered against his chest.

Their couple bond would heighten his senses, giving him some of the perception that a shifter had. Most importantly to Sara, it would give him the longevity to always be her mate. That mattered more to her than senses and the ability to see better, smell better, hear better. She already knew Joe had strengths that were paranormal in that area, strengths he'd gotten from his grandfather. The thing she valued the most, the longevity.

She couldn't imagine life without Joe. Ever. A thought came to mind. "Joe, I need you to make me a promise."

"What's that?" He stroked her hair, wrapping a lock around his fingers.

"You need to promise me you won't try to retaliate against Crossroads."

"I can't promise that. Not with all I know."

"Not good enough. I won't risk losing you by having you seek them out and hunt them down."

"Best I can say is I won't go looking for a fight, but I won't back down if one's brought to me."

Sara raised her head and looked into his eyes. The steely glint in them let her know there was no backing down for Joe on this one.

If that was the best he could offer, she'd take it. She knew his motivation. She planted a kiss on his jaw.

"I love you," he whispered, a vulnerability in his voice that his stoic face would never give away. It was nice to hear it. "I'll never let you go," he added.

"You'll never need to." With her head on his chest, she listened to the strong, rhythmic beat of his heart, beating in time to her own.

EPILOGUE

A week later...

Sara appraised Joe as he helped her out of his truck, something he insisted on doing. She knew it gave him pleasure, so why not let him? He'd cleaned up, put on a pair of pants other than jeans, and pulled his hair into a low ponytail. If she had to confess to it, she'd easily admit that she liked him straight from the forest, hair loose, flowing, just like his spirit did, wearing the grubby jeans that clung way too tightly in all the right places when he was turned on.

"What?" He raised a brow. "What are you looking at?"

"You." She reached up and kissed him.

"Happy?"

"More than I ever thought I could be."

"You don't care that I don't need a mansion or a fancy car? You're good with my cabin, the woods, and the simple life?"

Nothing about this man she loved was simple. Uncomplicated, yes. Simple, not a chance. He was the most amazing man she'd ever met. He was one with the forest and could see things she'd never been able to, even in her bear form. He said he was just like his grandfather. His grandfather must have been one hell of a man. Joe told her he'd been a Speaker. She knew very little about that stuff, but if Joe's connection to the forest was any indictor, she was in awe of his grandfather, the one they'd called Old One.

"Joe, I've never cared about that materialistic stuff." She doubted she could express to him how little any of that mattered when she was lying in bed next to him, her body flushed, her breathing and pulse erratic from his love. Or how she felt when he brought her coffee and made pancakes in the shapes of forest animals for Ivan. Or the way he taught Ivan how to throw a tomahawk with precision. Ivan would have the best of both worlds —shifter and Speaker.

"Ready?" he asked.

She smoothed her dress. Everyone was getting together for dinner at Grant and Chelsea's place. She hadn't met Grant or Chelsea yet; they were the only two from Bear Canyon Valley she'd yet to meet. They'd extended their honeymoon, and now they were back and had invited everyone to dinner.

Ivan had spent the night at Marti and Tanner's with Marti's son Dominic, whom Ivan was already calling a cousin. Tanner's truck was outside, meaning Ivan was already here.

Joe took her hand and helped her up the grand staircase. Their house was impressive. More like a mansion, really, and it was almost out of place in the beauty of the woods, yet somehow the architecture, the wood, the layout of the entire building made it work. It resembled a fortress, and knowing the history of the valley and shifter territory disputes, Sara wondered if it hadn't been used for exactly that.

The door opened, revealing a handsome man with a curvy, full-figured woman next to him. Both were beaming. Definitely the recently returned honeymoon couple. Their smiles were contagious.

Chelsea hugged Sara, meeting them on the landing before they could make it to the door.

"I'm so happy." She squeezed Sara in a tight embrace. "Joe deserved someone wonderful."

Sara's joy swelled inside her chest at the welcome.

Joe stood and raised his glass. "Cheers to the return of Chelsea and Grant."

They all raised their glasses.

Grant stood. "Cheers to a wonderful new addition." He coughed. "New additions, Sara and Ivan. And to one of my best friends finally having someone."

Astra rose. "Kane and I bought tickets for Europe. I'm going to find Anya. Mae said she'd been visiting Vax's brother."

Across from Astra, Doc rose to his feet. "I bought a ticket to Europe as well."

Mae paled. "What?"

Outside the windows, the sky went suddenly dark. A crack of thunder preceded a lightning flash.

"You can't." Mae's voice was low.

Another crack of thunder followed on the heels of her words.

Bear Canyon Valley was losing a shifter. And not just any shifter.

EXCERPT

Turn the page to keep reading the excerpt from *Attraction*...

Second chances are great.
Why doesn't sexy shifter Jake Evans, known to the Bear Canyon Valley shifters as Doc get it?

Mae's brewing up a storm. She's successful at finding mates for all the shifters in the valley.

All but one. The one she's in love with.

CHAPTER 1

A crash of thunder preceded Mae as she stormed into her home. Before she slammed the door behind her, a flash of lightning lit up the sky, making a stunning backdrop for the olive-skinned, full-figured beauty.

Of all the damned nerve. She stomped her foot. Kicked at a chair's leg.

Ouch. Damn it. Why was she acting like a teenager?

Him.

It was all his fault.

How dare Jake... No, she corrected herself, she shouldn't be thinking of him as Jake. He was Doc to everyone else, and as many years as she'd known him she'd have thought that by now she'd become accustomed to that moniker.

But he'd always be Jake to her.

Jake.

The man she'd fallen in love with.

Correction: he was the shifter she'd fallen in love with. She'd thought after Brad had died that she'd never find love again. Her heart had been broken. She'd been content with the dream she had of rebuilding Bear Canyon Valley into the shifter community that it used to be.

She'd only been good friends with Jake... Doc... Oh, the hell with it. She couldn't call him Doc. Just couldn't. He'd always be Jake to her. Sexy, amazing, musclebound Jake, the bear shifter.

When she'd run into Jake again, he was a widower too. He'd been married to Astra's mother, who was killed in a shifter battle, leaving behind a little girl that Jake had had to raise on his own, his stepdaughter Astra. He'd buried Astra's mother and taken Astra to Florida, where he'd done a wonderful job of raising her. Then he'd come back to Bear Canyon Valley.

Mae smiled at the thought of Astra, who had gifts, just as Mae did. Not the same exact gifts, but supernatural gifts, just the same. She should look into Astra's gifts to see if she needed help, though she felt she was the last person who had a right to do so, since she'd ignored and avoided her own gifts for so long.

The rain outside subsided a bit as she thought of Astra.

"I have got to get control of my emotions, or I'm going

to create a flood in this valley," Mae muttered to no one in particular, since she had no company.

Well, no human or shifter company. She had her black cat, Zorina, but that wasn't the same. It wasn't like Zorina could talk.

How dare Jake decide he was going to go to Europe? How dare he leave her behind?

No, she told herself, *how stupid of me to fall in love with him.*

The rain began again. More torrential now, with thunder and lightning flashes punctuating her every dark thought.

She should have known better. Of course Jake only thought of her as a friend. Well, then, she was a shitty friend, because she'd slipped out of Grant's home without an explanation other than that she didn't feel well.

She's braved the hammering rain and wind, tears blinding her. And she'd come home.

To pout. To sulk. To cry.

She threw her purse onto the sofa. It bounced, and her tablet flew out and crashed to the floor, right on the tail of another boom of thunder.

That was followed by a knock on the door.

Who in the world would be knocking on her door after nine o'clock on a Friday night?

Of course, remembering that it was a Friday night

didn't help because then she thought about her standing Friday nights with Jake.

Guess those weren't dates so much as they were two friends going out, she mused bitterly as she headed toward the back door.

∼

JAKE LOOKED AROUND THE MOSTLY EMPTY TABLE IN GRANT and Chelsea's dining room. The help was picking up the plates gingerly and quietly, being careful not to disturb anyone. They obviously sensed the tension in the room.

"Wow. Guess I know how to break up a dinner party." He flashed a rueful grin at his stepdaughter.

"Doc... You didn't..." Astra's words trailed off.

Her beautiful, luminescent green eyes studied him as if he were a child. Astra had always called him Doc, though on rare occasions, she referred to him as Dad. Either name worked. He was the only father she knew, and she'd told him many times that he was the only father she wanted.

"What?" He shrugged. "All I said was that I was going to Europe too. And poof, there goes Mae. Poof, there go Tanner and Teague. Poof, damned near everyone cleared out."

Chelsea and Grant were sitting across from him at the long table. Chelsea was smiling at Astra in that way that women had, the way that said they knew what the other one was thinking and they agreed completely.

Jake turned toward Grant. "You have a clue what I did wrong?"

Grant shrugged. "I'm staying out of it."

Well isn't that just great. Jake rose. "Excuse me. I think I'm going to go out for a beer."

Grant laughed. "Yeah, like that's going to do anything."

True. Alcohol had no effect on shifters, but it would give Jake an excuse to get out of here and go somewhere to think. He knew exactly where he was heading to.

Astra rubbed her temples. Kane looked at her, concern on his face.

"Are you okay?" Doc leaned closer, listening to her pulse with his shifter hearing. It was weak, slow.

"Yes. Just a headache." Astra stopped rubbing and took a sip of water.

"She gets those far too often," Kane said. "And they're increasing in frequency and strength."

Astra laughed weakly. "Doctor Kane, I presume?" she teased him.

"I'm serious." Kane frowned, brows dipping on his stern face.

"It's fine. Probably the weather. Barometric pressure, or sinuses, or something." Astra waved him away with a smile.

Kane looked at Jake pointedly. Jake got it, without further instructions. He'd need to look into the situation.

Sheesh. He should ask Mae. Except she'd stormed off.

It was something he'd done. That much he'd figured out, but he wasn't sure exactly what.

CHAPTER 2

Mae opened the door and gasped at the drenched sight before her.

"Tanner. What are you doing here?"

Tanner, soaked after walking in the pouring rain between his truck and her front door, looked like a puppy that had been playing in puddles. A big, muscular puppy.

"Better question is, why are you opening the door without bothering to see who it is?" He frowned, and his handsome face with its trim beard was stern.

"Don't be silly. Who would be out here that could be a danger to me?"

The moment those words left Mae's mouth, she realized how stupid they were. She could easily think of several threats and dangers.

Chelsea's psycho ex, Derek.

Jeff, the unstable, stalker realtor who was hung up on Chelsea.

The rover shifters who had attacked Kane.

She looked down to keep Tanner from seeing the chagrined look on her face.

"But what are you doing here?" she persisted, holding the door wider and handing him a kitchen towel to dry his face with.

Teague stepped in behind Tanner, equally soaked, equally handsome, but with a clean-shaven face.

"Teague too? Did you call in the National Guard as well?" She made a show of looking behind them.

"Why would we do that?" Teague asked. "Didn't you just say that there's no one out here who could be a danger to you?"

She avoided answering that question on the same grounds that she hadn't answered the last one. "Where are Marti and Kelsey?"

"Kane and Astra are giving them a ride home. We wanted to check on you."

"Two big ol' bear shifters coming to check on me." She gave them the eye. "I don't think so. What gives?"

They looked at each other. Tanner went first. "Mae, you know we owe you. You helped us out when we needed you most."

Mae cocked her head. "And you wanted to make sure I was okay because..." She waved her hands, urging them to move forward with their explanation.

"You got pissed when Doc said he was leaving. You left in a huff. A somewhat subtle one, but still a huff. And then a storm happened."

"So you're thinking that I have something to do with the weather?"

"Come on, Mae. It's us." Teague said. "We know what you can do. We lived here. We saw the rain during times that other areas had drought."

"Coincidence," Mae harrumphed.

"Coincidence too, that every time you'd visit Brad's gravesite it would rain in the cemetery, and only the cemetery?"

Damn them. They were way too perceptive.

"You've known all along," she mused.

"Yes, ma'am," Tanner said. "And we haven't told a soul that you're an element caster."

"Why didn't you mention it a decade ago, or more?"

"Mae." Tanner put his arm around her. "You're like our older sister."

Teague winked at her. "Though when he was a teenager, Tanner did have a crush on you."

Tanner jerked his arm away and turned a deep red. "I was a kid. Damn."

Mae slapped Teague's arm playfully. "Don't embarrass your brother."

"On a serious note," Tanner added. "We would never

divulge your secrets. But we do know that Doc's announcement bothered you."

"That's my issue to deal with," she reassured the hunky bear shifters. "There's more you're not telling me. You know I'll find out."

"Fine." Teague caved first. "Kane found a scent."

She frowned. "A scent of what?"

"Kane thinks it's polar bear." Tanner's face was grave.

Marti, Tanner's mate, had a son who was a polar bear. Mae knew that Marti didn't want it getting out that she had a polar bear shifter child.

She shook her head. This wasn't good. First of all, it meant there was a trespassing shifter in their territory. Secondly, it made her wonder if there was a connection to Marti's son Dominic.

She reached for a teapot, wanting to keep her hands busy. She filled it with water and put it on the burner.

"Let me see. I'll call—" Good grief. She'd almost said Jake. She couldn't call him, anyway, because things had changed. They weren't as close as she'd always thought they were. He'd planned a trip to Europe without even mentioning it to her until it was a done deal.

"Let me do some thinking," she told them.

"Why don't we call Doc?" Tanner asked.

Clearly, like her, he knew that was the normal way things were done. They would call her or Jake and then she and Jake would get together and talk and come up with solutions.

"No. Don't go calling Doc." She set the table with three cups for tea. "The man has a trip to plan and suitcases to pack."

He's embarking on more than a trip. He's embarking on a new life. One that doesn't involve me.

CHAPTER 3

Jake parked his car in his driveway and jumped out. His home wasn't quite the mansion that Grant's family had, but he hadn't done poorly. He had built a successful practice in Florida, then made some investments and was well set up for life. His home was a brick and wood two-story that he'd bought when he first arrived. The driveway was empty since he lived alone, now that Astra was living with Kane.

It was dark outside; the moon was barely a sliver. That had no bearing on his mission. He shifted into his bear seconds after slamming the door shut. He needed to go out into the woods. He needed to roam, to think.

He might even need to settle a matter with his bear, if his bear would let him broach the subject.

Forty minutes, multiple trails, and a long run later,

Jake pulled to a lumbering stop. His bear was winded but happy to have had the exercise.

Jake shifted back to his human skin and sat on a stump. He broke a twig off a nearby bush, stuck it in the corner of his mouth and chewed.

Now can we discuss it?

His bear grunted.

I have every right to be confused. Everything I've ever known about being a shifter has been turned upside down. Everything I've been taught flies in the face of what I'm feeling now.

His bear was quiet.

I wish you'd argue with me.

Jake knew the bear wouldn't. He knew the bear wanted him to sort this out on his own.

How can Mae be my mate? We've both had other mates.

Jake shook his head. He didn't know why he was struggling with this so much. His bear insisted this was the way it was and not to fight it. But Jake had to fight it. He'd had his mate: Astra's mother, Anna.

Jake wondered what she'd say about the way he felt about Mae.

He knew. She'd say, *Be happy. You can't be unhappy for the rest of your life.*

He cast the twig into the bushes.

None of this mattered. Mae didn't want him. Brad had been Mae's true mate. She considered Jake a friend.

All the more reason for me to get the hell out of Bear Canyon Valley. Maybe he could forget Mae in Europe.

Her olive skin and dark hair. Full lips, full hips, and a sassy attitude.

He exhaled a sigh. It was pointless to be in love with her. Pointless trying to get over his guilt about being in love with her. It violated their friendship and tore him in half.

"Lot of good this outing did me," Jake castigated his bear. "You were supposed to help me reach a resolution."

His bear roared in his head, drowning out all the sounds in the forest, even drowning out his thoughts.

Jake's blood pressure was rising. He could feel it. What the hell was his bear thinking?

"Seriously?" He didn't bother mind-communicating with his bear, but he was so agitated he spoke the word out loud.

You think I'm being silly? That I should roll with it? What happens the moment I tell her how I feel about her? It will upset the dynamics of the valley. She's put a lot into rebuilding this valley. A few words from me could destroy our working relationship.

His bear went quiet.

Fine. Now you want to give me the silent treatment.

Wait a second. His bear smelled something.

With a quick creaking sound, bones and tendons, skin and flesh stretching, Jake shifted into his bear.

Whatever it was, the bear felt they'd handle it better in his form. Jake had learned not to argue.

Jake inhaled, his nostrils flared. His bear grunted and pawed at the forest's pine-needle-covered floor.

A scent wafted his way.

Bear.

Not one of the Bear Canyon Valley shifters. This was an unfamiliar scent; that much he could tell.

The scent was faint and it wasn't easy to discern any details from it. Maybe if he followed it through the forest he'd be better able to tell some details.

He raised his head, picked up a trace, followed it a few paces. Raising his head again, he sniffed. He snarled.

Polar bear.

Jake approached a tree and leaned into it. Definitely polar bear. Not just a regular polar bear, of course.

A shifter.

A male.

And it had rubbed right here.

On purpose? Marking territory? Surely he knew this was their territory.

Jake had never had any real contact with polar bears. The only one he knew was Dominic. Could this bear have something to do with Dominic? It seemed to be out of bounds to discuss Dominic's father with Marti. She veered the conversation away from that topic any time it was broached.

Jake followed the scent up a trail that led away from

town. He never picked up the scent of another bear, just that one, and when he reached the creek, it stopped. He scoured a mile up and down the creek's opposite bank but couldn't find another trace.

That meant the bear had gone through the creek. Who knew how many miles?

So he wants us to know he's here, but he doesn't want us to find him.

He'd ask Mae.

No, he couldn't. He shouldn't. He should find a way to do things without Mae.

Yeah, right. As if they hadn't been attached at the hip for a long time now.

She'd be better off without him around all the time. She'd find someone to make her happy. The last thing she needed was to be with a shifter again.

His bear snarled at him.

I can come up with more reasons for staying away if I need to.

His bear's snarl turned into a thunderous roar. He would not be denied his mate. His bear had decided that Mae was the one for them.

Okay, okay. Jake couldn't argue that. He was already in love with Mae, had been for a long time, but he had to do what was right for her, what was right for the valley's shifters.

Back to the polar bear.

Plan of action? What would he do?

Fuck if I know.

He'd come back in the morning. There was bound to be some sort of an answer to this by then.

Just a matter of looking, he told his bear. *We'll find the answer in the forest.*

AFTERWORD

Hope you enjoyed the excerpt of the next story in the in the Shifters Forever Series:
Attraction

Another hot shifter. Another sassy, bootylicious woman. Another sexy story!

Check out www.ellethorne.com for more of the Shifters Forever Worlds! There are more than forty shifter stories with their wonderful happily ever afters! And wait until you meet the witches of New Orleans, and the elemen-

AFTERWORD

tals of Colorado, not to mention the polar bears of New York and Russia. So many shifters! So many love stories! Enjoy!

THE SHIFTERS FOREVER WORLDS

SHIFTERS FOREVER SERIES

Are you ready for it?

I have a whole world full of shifters to share with you. I'm listing them here, in the suggested reading order, though I've tried to make it so that you can pick up anywhere in the series as we all have probably done that at one point or another.

Many of these are organized in box sets for savings. Be sure to visit www.ellethorne.com to see which box sets are out!

Where's the best place to start? Well, probably with SHIFTERS FOREVER.

THE SHIFTERS FOREVER WORLDS

SHIFTERS FOREVER starts the series off with grizzly bear shifters and their mates that steam up the pages in these swoon-worthy paranormal romances. From trespassers with hidden agendas to curvaceous women who are ready to take a chance, the stories in this collection will capture your heart.

- PROTECTION
- SEDUCTION
- PERSUASION
- INVITATION
- TEMPTATION
- ATTRACTION

ALWAYS AFTER DARK is a spinoff with the white tiger from Shifters Forever: Vax, born Vittorio Tiero. He's the one that helped Kane out during a shifter battle. Follow the Tiero family, a group of white tiger shifters, as they head to America to find love... and heart-stopping danger. Full of romance, suspense, and gritty drama, this red-hot collection is sure to entertain!

- CONTROVERSY
- TERRITORY
- ADVERSARY
- SANCTUARY

NEVER AFTER DARK is another spinoff that takes place in Europe. Here we visit cities along the Mediterranean and meet the old school Tiero white tiger shifters who are resistant to change.
- FORBIDDEN
- FORSAKEN
- FORGOTTEN
- FOREPLAY

ONLY AFTER DARK takes place in New Orleans. The Arceneaux shifters, led by Lézare, Vax's white tiger cousin—on his mother's side. The Arceneaux are the black sheep of the family. Lézare doesn't cave to public opinion. He dictates policy in the area he rules and he shuns old school European rules and regimes.
- DESIRABLE
- INSATIABLE
- COMBUSTIBLE
- UNDENIABLE

MORE ONLY AFTER DARK takes place in New Orleans. The Arceneaux shifters and the Matthieu witches wreak havoc and find love within this city set on the steamy Louisiana coastline.

- Inevitable
- Inescapable

~

BITTER FALLS FOREVER features Mae Forester's nephew Dane Forester, a freewheeling, sexy, successful, movie star who uses every role and every woman to escape and forget the heartbreak he left in Bitter Falls.
- Unbound

~

BARELY AFTER DARK features more of Mae Forester's nephews! Grizzly bear shifters steam up the pages in these swoon-worthy paranormal romances. From trespassers with hidden agendas to curvaceous women who are ready to take a chance, the stories in this collection will capture your heart.
- Cross
- Lance
- Judge

~

Ever After Dark introduces us to the white tigers you learned to love in Always After Dark, Never After Dark, and Only After Dark. See their heritage. Visit Giovanni Tiero and his brothers Federico and Tito. Get reacquainted with Isabel Tiero and meet her sister Capriana Valenti.

- STONEBOUND
- FORMIDABLE

SHIFTERS FOREVER AFTER follows a group of polar bears in New York. Russian and rumored to be mobbed up, they are a powerhouse of shifters, determining the fate of many on the East Coast. Mikhail Romanoff, Layla's father, runs this outfit with an iron fist. Layla's sexy cousin Malachi features prominently in this series.
- COMPLICATION
- FASCINATION
- MOTIVATION
- CAPTIVATION
- FLIRTATION
- INFATUATION

FOREVER AFTER DARK takes place in Denver, Colorado. Enter a world of secrets and forbidden love. Panther shifters who who share their worlds with elementals must decide who they can trust—and who they can't live without.

- Notorious
- Scandalous
- Delicious
- Perilous

UPCOMING SERIES:

Shifters Forever More
Finally After Dark

I do hope you'll be able to join me on this wonderful journey with our Shifters Forever Worlds Shifters and their mates!
Hugs, Elle!

To receive exclusive updates from Elle Thorne and to be the first to get your hands on the next release, please sign up for her mailing list.
Put this in your browser:

http://www.ellethorne.com/contact

MY PERSONAL GUARANTEE:
THIS WILL ONLY BE USED TO ANNOUNCE NEW RELEASES AND SPECIALS. AND TO GIVE MY WONDERFUL SPECIAL READERS A LITTLE GIFT.

THANK YOU!!!

For sales and news, sign up for the newsletter! Thank you for purchasing and downloading my book. Words can't express what it means to me. If you enjoyed this read, please remember to take a second to leave a review. I'd love to know what your favorite parts were.

Have you fallen for these wonderful characters?

The fun isn't about to stop. Make sure you sign up for the link to the newsletter.

THANK YOU!!!

If you want to visit with me personally, you'll find me on Facebook at **www.facebook.elle.thorne.**7

Hearing from you means the world to me. This would not be possible without you and your love for reading.

With much gratitude, I thank you!

ABOUT ELLE

SEXY. BOLD. WICKED

Elle Thorne spent almost as much time denying that she wrote romance as she has writing it. It took her a few years to stop being a closet romantic.

Originally from Europe, she wouldn't dream of living anywhere else but Texas. Unless it was another southern —translation: warm!—state. A southern European by birth, she wants to be near the water and the Mediterranean temperatures if possible.

Where does she like to hang out? Near a lake, a beach, preferably with a latte—extra shot of espresso, please! She's inspired by the everyday men who make dreams come true. She loves a roughneck, especially one with a callous or two on his hands. A man who knows how to fix a car, please a woman, and protect what's his.

Nothing less will do.

ELLE'S NEWSLETTER

To receive exclusive updates from Elle Thorne and to be the first to get your hands on the next release, please sign up for her mailing list.
Put this in your browser:
www.ellethorne.com/contact

MY PERSONAL GUARANTEE:
THIS WILL ONLY BE USED TO ANNOUNCE NEW RELEASES AND SPECIALS. AND TO GIVE MY WONDERFUL SPECIAL READERS A LITTLE GIFT.

Made in the USA
Monee, IL
02 December 2019